BROTHER
of
DARKNESS
and Light

JEFF THOMPSON

TABLE OF CONTENTS

PROLOGUE

Hearken, my friends, to a tale of ancient days. This is a tale that comes from the dark and misty past; from the Age of Magic. It concerns the end of an age, and the beginning of a new age. As one age draws to a close, another more vital one begins.

Long ago there was a great conflict between the powerful forces of Good and Evil. Many were the victims of this struggle, as it lasted almost one hundred years. The carnage that was witnessed by all of the races of Erathyn was terrible indeed to behold.

In a fastness of the frozen North of the land, far beyond the pitiless Kharden Mountains, there lay the Tower of Malkaar. This sorcerer was the living embodiment of Darkness. It was he who had slain the many protectors of Erathyn in the pursuit of the forbidden knowledge of the Black Arts.

Down in the valley below the tower, immobilized in grotesque postures, were two armies, those of Darkness and of Light. The Army of Light had been gathered from all of the Kingdoms and lands of Erathyn. There were true Men, doughty Dwarves from the mountains, and tall, slim Elven warriors whose silver and gold armour flashed in the winter sun. Afoot and mounted on battle horses, they stood silently.

Above the army were suspended figures that were like Men with wings, which had the noble heads of hunting eagles. They hovered above the scene of battle, their small bows and slings had sent their deadly missiles ripping into the Army of Darkness. Some of those shafts had found their mark, but others hung in midair like hail that had been halted in mid-flight. Their chests were deep and muscled; not heavily, for these warriors of the air needed to be light for their wings to support them in that medium. They were the Avianinn. The

Elves had Shaped them to be scouts and warriors who could fight in the sky. Clad only in loincloths, they spurned armour, for it was too heavy for them.

Below them, in amongst the other warriors who trod the soil, were forms that were a blend of Men with the faces of felines. They were mounted on huge flightless birds that were twice as tall as the tallest Elf. They wore leather armour, and wielded long swords, bows, and spears to deadly effect. They were the Felininn; feline warriors who had been Shaped by the Elves in the same way that the Avianinn had been. They had come from their island home that lay far away to fight for the freedom of Erathyn.

The Army of Darkness, however, consisted of the lowest dregs of humankind. There were also terrible creatures in its ranks, which were an unclean blending of Man and beast. These monsters were the result of black sorcery, and though some of the strange forms could be identified, many were just amorphous figures from nightmare. Among these were the Cobrans; those awful beings that were an unclean melding of snake and man, who were Malkaar's staunchest supporters. This entire evil host was clad in black, and hanging above it on long flagpoles were pennants that were blood red and venomous green.

The sorcerous struggle that had culminated in the valley had locked the two armies in stasis, mute testimony to the equilibrium of the contending forces that now could have no victor. Figures stood where they had been struck by the magic. Soundless screams and wordless exclamations were locked in a terrible still moment that would last for eternity. Figures which only moments before had been caught up in mortal struggle, stood immobile as statues. On horse or afoot, they seemed to be carved out of stone. Held in the very act of violence, they presented a strange tableau in their statuesque rigidity. The ground beneath them had been churned by the force of their strife. Mud and slush splashed all from head to foot. Blood had pooled like the finest red wine, mingling with the poisonous green ichor of the evil progeny of the cobra.

Here four Cobrans beset a Man. Anger and fear was clearly seen on his blood-spattered face as he realised he was about to die. There was an Elf who was down on one knee, who had a Cobran impaled upon his spear, raised high above his head. The snake-man's hands grasped the shaft; his mouth was wide open in a never-ending scream of pain. A Dwarf's axe had taken his foe's head from his shoulders with a dark spray of black blood. The Dwarf had cried out in exultation at his enemy's demise. An Avianinn had plunged from the sky, pierced with three black arrows. Feathers hung about him in a cloud. One of the Felininn had speared his enemy, and his mount had torn the arm from another. Next to him, a Felininn warriors mount had crashed to the ground, and several of the black clad enemy stood above him, their swords stabbing savagely. The crushing impacts, deep thrusts and hacking of weapons were expressed in the flower-like explosions of blood and splintering spears which hung in mid-air like some grotesque garden of death and destruction.

Warrior's arms were stilled in frozen positions; some clutched raised or falling weapons. Others were flung wide as they had received a fatal blow. All had become steel seedlings in that garden. Stiffened and blood-soaked rags, that once had been proud banners and flags of battle, resembled twisted branches as they stood above the halted, silent warriors. Rearing horses and struggling combatants alike were caught as if they were images in a tapestry that adorns a castle wall. Hundreds of arrows hung high in the air, and shot from a thousand slings hovered above the battlefield in an impossible cloud. A company of Elven bowmays stood with their bows drawn back to their cheeks in a volley that had not been released. But it was clear that the combined forces of Men and Elves had pushed the host of Malkaar back and Dwarven axes and war hammers had smashed through the press. The Elven mounted host had poured through the widening gap that had opened up, and the battle line of the Dark One's forces had collapsed under the shock of the assault. At the very moment when stasis had enthralled both armies, the Army of Darkness had been on the verge of defeat.

Leading the Elven horse was a tall figure mounted atop a fine Elven steed. Longsword raised high above her head, she was at the forefront of the advancing forces. Golden armour shone in the sun, and a long green cape billowed around her and her horse. Her hair flowed behind her like a golden mane, and a crown encircled her noble head.

She combined beauty and warlike spirit in equal amount; her graceful form was fair to look upon, and the fallen enemies that she had slain with her longsword who lay broken beneath her mount's hooves were mute testimony of her prowess in battle. Yet her face also showed that she was amongst the wisest of all of the Races of Erathyn. Her counsel would have been sought throughout the land. Keen her thoughts would be; as keen as her blade, and her words would have carried weight in any council gathering. She was Nerolynn, the Queen of the Elves; the perfect warrior woman who was without peer amongst them. Her mouth was frozen open, for when the spell had struck her down, she had been urging her forces to advance and destroy the enemy. Her blue eyes blazed defiance. Black blood fouled her blade to the hilt, and her armour was dented and splashed with gore. Her mount was spattered with blood and mud that had sprayed upward from the churned up ground. Surrounding Nerolynn were her finest mounted Elven warriors, male and female alike. They had broken through the foe's battle line, which had crumbled and scattered before them. Supported by Men and Dwarves, their horses could not be matched by the enemy, who had no mounted warriors. On either side of their queen, the mounted Elves had struck down any of the enemy in reach, their attack benefitting both from the height from which they struck, and from the irresistible rush of their mounts as they had slammed into the breaking ranks of the Dark One's forces. Bodies hung in mid-air, hurled there by the impact of the Elven horse. Helms and skulls alike had been split in sprays of dark blood by the longswords that the Elven warriors had wielded from atop their mounts. Dwarves had rushed forwards, their axes and war hammers and pure body weight lending an unstoppable impetus to the Elven breakthrough. Behind them had come Men; mounted and afoot, hastening to come to grips with the enemy. The Felininn had urged their mounts into the gap, the giant birds cruel beaks had snapped at the Dark One's retreating forces. Above them all, the Avianinn hung poised to hurtle down from the sky and pursue Malkaar's rabble into destruction.

Malkaar's army had fallen back in dissaray from the onrush of the mounted warriors; a retreat that looked like it would become a headlong rout. Even the Cobrans couldn't face the might of the Elven horse, and had been crushed under the flying hooves like all the rest. The Army of Darkness had disintegrated, its formations shattered and leaderless. The evil host that had overrun every village and city upon Erathyn and destroyed and laid waste everywhere it had set foot, was now in danger of being overrun itself by the vengeful forces that had been united from every race it had preyed upon. The broken and battered ranks had fallen back, pushed towards Malkaar's stronghold, the tower that stood tall and dark at the end of the valley.

And yet the destruction of that army had been brought to a timely halt by the sorcerer's use of the Spell of Stasis. Malkaar had chosen to sacrifice his forces to stop the Army of Light from defeating his army, and taking and killing him. Frozen in time, the two contending armies stood mutely, statues in a moment of unnatural stillness.

Above this grim and fantastic scene the Tower of Malkaar loomed in the mist, like some forbidding sentinel on the shores of dream and nightmare. An imposing edifice it was, made of a dark stone which gleamed with a reddish glow reminiscent of a smouldering coal that lay in darkness.

Within the tower, Malkaar regained his strength slowly. He spawled in his ebon throne, which was made from the warped and twisted bones of enemies that his vile sorcery had slowly drained of life. These he had shaped to form a mockery of a cleaner, more natural seat. Such was his bitter and twisted humour, and his contempt for all who opposed him in his quest for ultimate power. Malkaar was a very old Man. He was one hundred and eighty years of age. This weighed heavily upon him, despite his sorcerous means of sustaining his vigour. His face was fearful to look upon, for he radiated evil in a dark and intense gaze, much in the same way a snake will hypnotize its prey. Malkaar's icy stare, however, was not as natural as this was. His eyes seemed to leech the very life out of whomever he looked upon. He wore a robe as black as midnight, covered in the symbols of Dark Magic, as befitted a master of the forbidden arts. The sorcerer's face was thin and drawn. One could say he was emaciated, with sunken cheeks and a pallor of skin only found in one who spends most of his life shunning the sunlight. His hands were two bony claws. Weirdly elongated, his crooked fingers seemed like the legs of great white bony spiders.

With head in hand, he sat in great weariness, for this day would have seen the timely destruction of the great and terrible army in his service, which had long been a curse upon the lands that they had sought to conquer in his name. Only his Spell of Stasis had halted his army's defeat, and his remaining powers could not work upon objects thus set outside time. The forbidden sources to which he owed his terrible vitality were sapped, although he was still a dreadful opponent.

The darkened room in which he sat was at the very heart of the tower. Bones and horribly suggestive profiles of faces and limbs hung about these walls, with many other strange objects. There were ornate wooden spears, covered with strange sigils and stained with blood. Great tapestries hung on the walls, aswirl with bizarre cabalistic designs. There were also masks of Dark Magic design, and dried, leathery snake skins. On a table which had legs carved like leering gargoyles stood beakers and retorts, mortar and pestle and other instruments of the necromantic arts; pots with questionable contents, all outlines blurred by a sifting of fine dust. A ruddy light flickered over all, provided by a few fluttering torches in wall sconces. A foul musty reek hung in the air, like the smell of some long-dead reptile. Only his harsh breathing disturbed the stillness of the darkened chamber.

Outside, in the howling wasteland, the unrelenting winds of an imminent storm lashed the faces and chilled to the bone a small group of Elves, who stood upon a hill overlooking the battlefield and the tower. They were the only survivors from the Army of Light who had escaped the spell in the valley. They were tall and slim, with the otherworldly beauty of their race. There were seven in this small group; one could tell by the deference shown to the oldest and only female among them that she was their undisputed leader.

Her figure was wrapped in a robe so stained with blood, mud, and other unidentified matter that one could not be sure of its original colour. Her face expressed a kindly and serene nature, blended with a look of great wisdom. Her ageless visage was marked with the stress and strain that she had undergone in the magical combat with Malkaar. She had long been his worthy opponent. She leaned on a great carven staff, which had many mystic runes burned into the heart of its living wood by High-Elven magic. Her long blonde hair moved as if alive, whipped about by the bitter wind.

This, then, was Shaarla, the last surviving member of the Council of Light, the enclave of Elven wizards who were dedicated to uphold the forces of good in Erathyn. She had participated in the battle against Malkaar's army this day, but she knew that until Malkaar himself was dead or wholly bound by a spell, there would be no peace. The Army of Light had been on the verge of defeating Malkaar's host when he had cast his spell. She knew that it had been a last resort on his part. Her almond-shaped eyes; eyes that had seen many terrifying and wonderful things, looked with a keenness impossible for one not of her race, down at the tower which contained her old enemy. Drawing a painfully cold breath, she faced the dread task that she alone must complete. She well knew that the only way to bind Malkaar was to evoke the most powerful magic, which would take her own life in its process.

"Let it be so then," she said to herself, counting her life as small price to pay for the end of the threat to Erathyn. She had lived long, but all things must end, even sometimes the everlasting lives of the Elves. For although they were immortal, and age did not weary them like Men, they could be slain in battle.

"Your pardon, Mistress?" queried one of the group.

Turning, she saw the concerned faces of the young acolytes. She looked keenly into each face, seeing the love and respect that was in their eyes. But she also noted the fear of the unknown future. She came over to where they huddled shivering, and placed her hands on the shoulders of two of them. They were obviously brothers. She looked each of them in the eye.

"Boka, Arnath, you must both be strong. Malkaar has stopped our army, but only at the cost of his own. All that remains is the final stroke, and I must deal it." Their breath smoked in the frosty air as they listened.

Shaarla looked around at the other four, no less her honoured pupils. Jerin, who was quietly resolute; Kolar, who did not say much but was a good pupil. Eskyn, who was the opposite of Kolar in all except talent; smiling, always friendly and cheerful. And Kerith, the wisest and eldest of them though barely eighteen. In many ways she looked upon him as her own son.

"The King's force has not appeared, and I fear the worst. The Dark One must have destroyed them." She stood for a moment, as if listening. "I cannot sense him or any of his companions, nor indeed any living thing, good or evil, in the High Pass. We can wait for them no longer. Malkaar must be nearly spent if he must sacrifice his own army to stop us."

"What do you intend to do, Mistress?" Eskyn said.

"I shall call down the Ice of Foreverness. You, Kerith, take the vowed six to Algol and safety. You cannot help me."

Kolar gasped. The others gave a chorus of disapproval.

"But what of the Queen?" Boka said.

"The Queen is lost," Shaarla said. "The spell has taken her from us. But we cannot allow the Dark One to escape. The Ice of Foreverness is the only way to ensure he is stopped. I will make the spellcast while you return to Algol."

Kerith shook his head.

"The Dark One will sense what you are doing and stop you. We will distract him. If you fail, we will not be safe at Algol or anywhere on this world." Shaarla could see the determination on his face and knew that he would not be denied.

"It is the only way, Mistress," added Kolar.

Shaarla held each of them in her gaze for a few moments.

"Go then, vowed companions, and as you go remember your fallen friends and families. Remember what Erathyn would have become had the Dark One succeeded with his foul designs."

They all understood. If they went down to the dark stronghold and faced the Dark One, they would go to their deaths, either from him or from his sorcery. Even if any of them survived the combat with Malkaar, they would still be locked in the ice with him. None of them would return.

"We serve the Council and all Erathyn, Mistress," said Kerith, striving to control his fear by a show of determination. To his credit, he did passably well. It is not an easy thing to know of one's impending death, and to go doggedly to meet it. Even Elves, who were taught from birth to control their emotions, sometimes allowed those emotions to show.

To a Man, this display would seem very strange. They thought that the Elves had no emotions. Only at a time of great stress such as this would anyone see an inkling of their inner thoughts.

"I honour you all," Shaarla said. She bowed to them.

Kerith returned her bow, and motioning to the others, turned to go. They all bowed before her. As one they turned and made their way down to the tower, a gesture of ultimate sacrifice. Eskyn went first, then Jerin, the impassive Kolar, Boka and his brother Arnath, and lastly, Kerith. Shaarla leaned on her staff and watched them go, until she lost them in the swirling flurries of snow. Then she lifted her arms wide, and looking not at the sky, but beyond it, she began the spell.

Malkaar lifted his head from his hands. An evil smile writhed around his aged and leathery lips. His eyes held a dark and unfathomable hint of other dimensions. His face was blank. His mind was wandering amid the trackless star-reaches as in a drug-induced dream. Then a look of new awareness passed across his face, as a frigid wind will race across a pond in winter, whirling the snow upon the ice in its passage. He spoke, his voice as harsh as the rasp of rusty metal echoing in the sepulchral room.

"Ah. Visitors."

Eskyn died swiftly. A blazing fireball blasted him when he stepped out of the corridor. The deadly magic of Malkaar had been unleashed. He stood in the centre of the room, a baleful nimbus of Darkness swirling around him, as a whirlpool rushes and spins. His arms were held high, his hands cupped to hold the frightful energies he was ready to cast. The sorcerer's mocking leer as he confronted the young acolytes proclaimed the simple fact that they were no match for his dreadful power. Unnatural fires flickered in his eyes, changing from yellow to orange like flames.

"Welcome," he said with a voice that was terrible to hear. "Your most strongest of magicks are as nothing when compared to my sorcery. You are motes of dust in the winds of eternity, and you shall be swept into oblivion." With a triumphant leer, he cast another ball of fire.

Shaarla had completed her opening cast and was intensifying the great intrusion of the Ice of Foreverness. Her jaws were set in a grimace of pain. The fearful struggle of the casting showed on her face as sweat beaded there. Her eyes were glazed over as she chanted the alien words. The runes on her staff burned with the power she invoked. Most of her mind was concentrated on ensuring the spell was successful, but she still had a tenuous grip of reality on her own plane. She sensed Eskyn's death and knew it was but the first. The lowering sky had turned from a dirty grey to a howling miasma of bright, electrifying blues and greens. A great vortex of clouds was approaching rapidly.

Within the tower, the acolytes hurled ravening beams of huge destructive power at the Sphere of Darkness that Malkaar had summoned to shield himself. To the eye it looked unbearably hot; sparks and flashes of fire ringed it all about. The room grew stifling as they all concentrated their energies upon it, and breathing became very difficult. The terrible bombardment stopped. Instantly a tongue of black flame licked out of the sphere, and three of the acolytes ceased to exist. The sphere faded, and Malkaar stood before them again, ready to deal death instantly. The smell of burned flesh was ambrosia to his nostrils, which flared as a wild beast's do when scenting its quarry. Kerith and Boka remained facing him resolutely. The pain of the loss of his younger brother was written on Boka's face, yet he stood facing their grim adversary. Kerith realised that if Shaarla's spell were to work, Malkaar's concentration must be kept fully on them, or else his heightened senses would detect Shaarla's magic, and all would be lost. He held his hands up in a gesture of surrender.

"Malkaar!" he cried, "Have done! We are no match for such a mighty one as you. Spare us to be your slaves and we will do your bidding."

The Dark One paused and seemed to consider.

Out in the screaming winds, Shaarla sensed what Kerith planned. She completed the casting, and pointed her staff at the cloud that hovered over the tower. The cloud began to descend in a howling, lightning-shot mass of energy that shrilled deafeningly. Inside, the sorcerer smiled, relishing his moment of supreme power over the two acolytes. Without warning, he sent a jet of black flame at the lesser of his two enemies. Boka died without a sound as Malkaar turned to face Kerith who stood there with his hands still raised in submission.

"I don't need you, foolish Elf. I am the ultimate power of Darkness. Begone!" With that, he cast a fireball at Kerith, who stood there defenceless. Even as he died, Kerith's last thought was that Shaarla would be completing the casting, and that he and his companions sacrifice had not been in vain. Malkaar began to laugh, gloating over his easy victory. His laughter began as a deep evil chuckle, rising in pitch and energy, until he fairly shrieked with unholy glee, spinning around the chamber with his robes flying around his capering figure.

Shaarla sensed Kerith's death. She cried the final Word of Power with her last strength, then lowered her staff to the ground and leaned on it, her breathing ragged. The shuddering, moaning cloud of energy descended upon the tower. It rimed the outer walls with frost, which hardened into ice with supernatural speed. Layer upon layer of it swathed the tower, until its outline was indistinct. The reddish glow about the tower dimmed and flickered. Shaarla could feel her very life force draining from her body as the spell sucked it from her. She swayed drunkenly as she stood there watching the forces which she had summoned from Outside at work.

Inside, the massive rents in the very fabric of the plane, and the powerful Summoning alerted Malkaar too late, and he sensed the presence of Shaarla.

"NO!" His throat convulsed with a scream, as he realised that he had been distracted in a fatal moment. Too late, he understood the sacrifice of the acolytes. Even as he thought this, the cloud enveloped the tower. It all solidified into a huge block of impenetrable ice. He felt his body begin to stiffen. He stumbled painfully around the chamber, casting fireballs at the encroaching ice, which melted briefly and reformed in ever thickening layers on the walls. The torches, guttering in the chill, went out. The electric blue glow of the ice replaced their light. Malkaar tried to move, but found that he was frozen to the floor, and looking down in fury, discovered that his frigid doom was encroaching rapidly up his legs. His frantic struggles were to no avail, so he cast several spells in quick succession. They had no effect. The room itself around him grew smaller and smaller until he was watching the ice creep upward across his chest. The absolute cold of the star-spaces pervaded his being. As his final breaths froze, he screamed a last animal scream of defiance, the sound of which was swallowed up by the ice as it enclosed him in its frigid grip.

Outside, the snowstorm spun and tossed about the dying wizardess, murmuring with her last breath, as if to her staff, "It is done." A faint smile wrote itself across her face. The light left her eyes. She dropped her staff as she slumped forwards.

She fell face-first into the snow, which covered her in a while, for with the completion of the magic, the weather resumed as if nothing unnatural had occurred. Down in the valley, the two armies remained locked in strife. Inside the Ice of Foreverness, the figure of Malkaar stood within his frigid prison. His hate-filled eyes stared at nothing. The tower remained locked in the ice's chill embrace, a final symbol of the terrible conflict between Elven magic and black sorcery.

Nine hundred years after these events took place; a strange figure appeared on the hill of the spellcast. Dressed in a forester's green tunic, worn and tattered, he hummed tunelessly to himself as he stooped and collected firewood. His arms seemed too long for his bowed and twisted body. The way in which his clothing hung loosely betrayed that he was a hunchback. Long, lank blond hair blew in the breeze around his sun-tanned and leathery face, which was as twisted as his body. His eyes held no hint of intelligence, only seeming to fill their sockets in his vacant face. He bent and picked up an unusual piece of wood, long and straight, that had strange markings on it.

He stared at the markings, not realising that they were High-Elven runes. At the edge of his hearing, he seemed to sense a melodious sound that rose and fell faintly. He listened closely; it was as though the wood itself was singing. He cocked his misshapen head to one side and attempted to hum along with the melody. As he did so, the sound dwindled and faded away. Frowning, he shook the stick, but its song didn't return. He turned the wood over in his hands and shrugged.

He looked across the valley to where the imprisoned tower was locked in the Ice of Foreverness and scratched his head. The meaning of it all was far too much for him to comprehend. He had been down to the valley, but the two armies, locked in rigid combat, and the ice-covered tower itself were beyond his understanding, so he eventually ignored them.

He added Shaarla's wooden staff to the rest of his firewood and returned to his hut, which lay not far away. This was a ramshackle collection of odd-shaped and miss-matched timber, which obviously had been scrounged in much the same way as his firewood had been. This he placed on the dirt floor near the fireplace, and began to fill a battered old pipe. Then he prepared the fire and lit it.

He was alarmed at first when the unusual bit of wood gave off an icy blue glow in the fireplace. His eyes opened wide, and he stared dumbly. The heat of the fire seemed to suddenly die, and a bitter chill invaded the hut, as everything was flooded in cold blue light. He backed away from the fire with his mouth agape, as he watched the flames stealing along the wood. Suddenly, the song came again. This time it began as a wail, and then slowly turned into a harsh scream that made him block his ears. He moaned in pain as it throbbed in his head. Bright rays of light flared from the runes as the fire ate them. But then there was a sharp crack, and the glow faded to be replaced by the normal warmth and light of the flames. He lowered his hands cautiously as the sound died away. He crept forward to peer at the wood, but now it was just a blackened stick curling in the flames. After a while, it burned normally with a pleasing smell, so he picked up a glowing taper, and lit his pipe. Then he settled back in his old chair and promptly forgot all about it. Eventually, he slipped into slumber in the pleasant heat of the hut. His pipe fell to the floor and went out. His snores mingled with the crackling of the fire.

Outside, down in the valley, amid the immobilized armies, the tower had stood locked in the ice, even when the snows had come and gone, following the seasons as they must in an unending cycle since time immemorial.

The ice began to melt...

CHAPTER I

THE DARKNESS RETURNS

"His Majesty wishes us to rejoin our people. He believes that we should be one again before the return to Glindarion." The speaker was a tall Elf-lord clad in a shimmering white robe which had a silver and gold pattern worked upon it in Elven design. A circlet of gold was on his head, denoting his rank. In his hands he held a scroll, which he had been reading from. His face held no signs of age, seeming neither young nor old. His hair was like living gold, which fell to his waist. He looked up at the others around him. His name was Malor, the Lord of Oakdean.

Two women stood there; one young and beautiful, and with hair as long and as golden as his was, for she was his daughter, the Lady Elinor. Her dress was made of fine stuff like her father's robe, and she had eyes of the clearest blue, which sparkled with intelligence.

The other woman was older; although like Malor, her face was ageless and serene. She wore the brown robes of a healer, and the only ornament about her person was a small *firestone* hung from a leather cord around her neck. Her brown hair was long as well, but was plaited to keep it out of her way as she practised her craft. She was called Shelarindel.

One other stood there; the Elf-lord Nildoron. He was the King's messenger who had brought the scroll to Oakdean. He was dressed in forest green and wore a long riding cloak and tall boots. His hair was as brown as the healer's, and tied back from his face. He wore a golden torc about his neck, which was covered with High-Elven script, indicating that he was the King's messenger. He waited for Malor to speak again.

They were all tall and fell and fair to look upon, as all the Elves were. They had the pointed ears of their kind, and almond-shaped slanted eyes. Their cheekbones were high and rounded, in faces that were smooth and without blemish. Their voices were fair and musical.

They stood upon a balcony in the City of Oakdean, which lay on the Silvering River's banks. The city was made with the Shaping magic of the Elves from the trees of the forest, for they revered them and would cut no living wood. It was made up of many towers and halls, which looked like nothing so much as sculptures of ethereal beauty. Pinpoints of light flashed here and there as the rising sun picked out windows. The trees flowed together and formed the buildings; white was the overall colour, with the life-giving sap coursing through them. This gave the city the look of white marble with green veins; however, unlike that precious stone, it pulsed with a warm life of its own.

The river could be heard flowing below them with an unceasing and ever-changing music. The sound of birds rang across the air. All was peaceful and tranquil. The morning sun was rising through the mist. The sounds of harp and Elven pipes was heard from within. The group had come from the banqueting hall to discuss the message in private. It was early Spring, and they had been breaking their fast when Nildoron had arrived.

"Perhaps it is time, Malor," said Shelarindel. "We have dwelled here for many years, and all know that we shall go back home soon. The Age of Magic is coming to a close, and this world will belong to Men."

The Lord of Oakdean rolled up the scroll and handed it back to Nildoron. A distasteful look came upon his face.

"It is because of Men that we live here apart from our people, and when we are gone, this world will fall into chaos and disorder, for Men have no idea of the true nature of things; they are greedy and weak, each lusting after his brother's possessions. They cannot control their emotions, and grasp land and cut down the forests needlessly for their farms. Wherever Man goes, he destroys." He turned to look out across the river, thinking of better times. "They are like children."

"In their innocence, children sometimes do wicked things," offered Shelarindel.

Malor turned to look at her. "They are *not* innocent. The Dark One was a Man. He stole the secrets from our wizards at Algol and turned them against us. It was because of him that the War of the Races came about. It was because of him that many died." *Including my wife*, he thought.

Elinor saw the brief pain in his face and stared down at the floor, she did not want to meet his eyes. Death to the immortal Elves was indeed a bitter thing.

The healer shook her head. "Not all Men are evil. There is good and bad in all races. You cannot say that all Men are the same, even as all Elves are not the same."

Elinor came forward. "It is true, Father. I have met Men and Dwarves, and they are as different to each other as we are. Some are noble and good, others bad."

He was about to reply when Nildoron spoke.

"The King has not sent me to speak of Men, my lord. He asks only that you will rejoin us. The sundering of our people lies heavily upon his mind, and he wishes us to be one again." He knew that it would not be easy to persuade Malor. The Elves of Oakdean had remained apart from the Elven kingdom for a long time, and Nildoron knew of Malor's stubbornness.

Ignoring Nildoron, Malor spoke to Elinor.

"I know of the ways of Men, daughter. I fought by their side in the War. I have seen first-hand what they are like. Sometimes when we defeated the enemy and re-took a city, they robbed from the dead and quarrelled amongst themselves over the spoils. "

"That does not mean that they are all bad, Father. The Men who fought to destroy the Dark One and free Erathyn were good Men. The Union of Races had good people; Elves and Dwarves *and* Men."

Lord Nildoron interjected. "There is another matter, my lord."

Exasperation showed on Malor's face. His daughter was becoming more and more outspoken as the days went by. He addressed Nildoron.

"Yes?" he asked.

The messenger took a deep breath. This would be difficult, but it was the King's order, and Lord Nildoron was pledged to do the

King's will. "His Majesty also wishes that you and your brother be reconciled."

Silence fell. The little group waited for Malor's reaction.

"I *have* no brother," he said grimly.

Shelarindel began, "But Goldwen—"

"Speak not to me of him. He received what he desired; to be the Eldest. That means more to him than I do." His face was like a stone.

"That is not true, Father," said Elinor.

The Lord of Oakdean turned to her. "Leave us, daughter," he said sternly.

Elinor looked at Shelarindel, who shook her head slightly. Elinor looked upon her as a mother, and it was clear that she did not wish the maiden to defy her father. Elinor bowed, and left the balcony.

Lord Malor watched her depart. He was embarrassed that Elinor had caused a scene in front of the King's messenger. "I apologize, my lord," he said to Lord Nildoron. "My daughter is headstrong, and she must learn her place."

"I understand, my lord. She has strong feelings for—"

Malor held up his hand in a gesture of silence.

"Now it is I who must apologize, my lord," said Nildoron. "His Majesty was adamant about this. He cannot see that we can be one people if you will not renew your relationship with your brother."

"I agree, my lord," added Shelarindel. "It is foolish to continue this animosity. The War has long been over, and it is time to change."

"Change? We Elves do not change. Only in the world around us is there change. We go on for eternity, the immortality of our race making the other lesser races fear and despise us. Would that we *could* change, perhaps then we would truly understand the ways of Men."

Lord Malor turned and leaned on the railing. He stared across the river into the mountains that faded into the mist. He spoke as though to himself.

"I blamed him for many years and for many things. I blamed him for the War, and also for my wife's death. He turned away from us to devote himself to the Council. When all thought he had died in the

Last Battle, I rejoiced. Now I know that I was wrong." He stared out at the rising sun.

Nildoron and Shelarindel stood silently, not wishing to interrupt his reflection. Soon, however, Lord Nildoron would want an answer to take back to the King. He hoped it would be the right one.

Elinor, her face a blank mask, walked quickly across the banqueting hall and down the corridor. All who saw her pass realised that she had quarrelled with her father, and wisely did not attempt to stop her.

He treats me like a child, she thought. *It is unfair. All I spoke was the truth. Why does he hate Men so? Is it because of Mother?*

Lost in her thoughts, she wandered along the corridor down to the greeting hall. Suddenly, she felt a chill, as though a cold wind had touched her.

"Elinor. . ."

A cold voice whispered to her. Startled, she looked around. No one was there. Her glance traversed the hall. Then, at the front doors that stood at the far side of the room, she could see a dark shape all hooded and cloaked.

"Who are you?" she demanded.

The figure did not reply. Turning, it walked out of the doors and proceeded outside. Elinor, her curiosity raised, and perhaps a little angry that she was not answered, followed.

As she came outside, she looked around for the form, and saw it disappear down a path, which led through the gardens and down to the river. She went after it.

Up on the balcony, Lord Malor saw his daughter pass along the path below, but did not see what she was pursuing. He would have to speak to her about her manners, once his business with Lord Nildoron was concluded.

"If it is His Majesty's will, I shall contact my brother," he said, "Although I believe he thinks his work at Algol is far more important than reconciliation with me."

"Do not be so sure, my lord," said Shelarindel. "Goldwen is very busy, but I know he still has great love for you, and would surely wish to do the King's bidding."

"Perhaps," Malor said doubtfully.

Elinor had passed through the gardens in pursuit of the phantom. She came to a small glade. The trees waved gently in the breeze, letting in brief rays of the morning sunlight that shone in the fine dust-motes that glittered about her. The intermittent rays pierced the green and cool light of the glade, which looked as if it could have been underwater; so tranquil and peaceful it appeared. The apparition was nowhere to be seen.

The river lay before her. She walked down to it, knelt at its edge and cupped the water in her hands to drink. The water was cool and good, and she could feel its coolness soothe her throat as she drank. She wondered where the figure had gone. What was it? Was it a Sending, such as the wizards used?

At that moment, she felt the chill again, but this time it was as if an icy hand had grasped her in a vice-like grip and drained the heat from her vibrant young body. She knelt there, shivering with the cold. Water dripped from her trembling hands into the river. As the ripples spread, they broke up the image of a dark shadow that reached for her from the opposite bank. Shaking with the supernatural cold that had descended upon her, she stared at the reflection on the river. Looking up, she saw that it was the shape she had been following.

It stood motionless, its right hand grasping a staff. The figure was staring at her, and Elinor, struck dumb with fear, could feel its dread presence. It lifted the staff, and floated straight across the river towards where she knelt paralysed. The shape swiftly became larger in Elinor's sight, as though it had been dropped from the sky directly above her, and was falling straight into her face. She could only gasp wildly for breath, and stare in mute terror at the oncoming apparition. Her heart crashed in her ribs as she struggled vainly to free herself from the icy grasp. The shadowy thing halted before her, and with it came a coldness so bitter as to make the first chill seem almost pleasant. The cold enveloped her like an unseen mist from the far North. Her breath smoked as it would on a winter morning as it left her panting lips.

The spectre hung there in terrible silence. Elinor could see no face at all, and noticed for the first time that the figure was dim and wavering as though seen from a great distance; only the general shape could be made out. Suddenly, she could see two flaming eyes, as though a fire had kindled within the cowl. The staff was extended towards her, and a low, guttural voice spoke in an alien tongue, speaking a spell. At once, the pressure of the grip increased, and her breathing became even more rapid. Sweat, despite the frigid chill, started out of her pores. The voice continued monotonously. Runes of power burned in a black fire that twined about the staff. She felt herself lifted from the ground by an unseen force, and was suspended in the air before the shadowy shape. A nimbus of light surrounded her, gradually becoming brighter than the sun. All other sounds faded away from her awareness as she hung there. Just as she felt that she would be crushed to death by the unrelenting pressure, it lessened; there came a sharp, tearing pain. A fire seemed to come from her belly and spread through her body, even to the ends of her hair, which stood out with sparks dancing in it. She felt an alien life within her, impossibly growing. Her blood burned in her veins with a fierce heat. Elinor regained her voice. Throwing her head back, she screamed once, long and high, as though all of the pain of the whole world had found a voice, then she fell into a deep darkness and knew no more.

On the balcony above, the three who stood there heard her scream. They looked at each other in surprise. Awareness showed in Malor's face. *"Elinor!"* he cried. As one, they left the balcony and hurried into the hall.

Passing through the now deserted banqueting room, they hastened down the corridor, through the greeting hall, and outside, where they saw a group going down the path in the direction that Elinor had taken. They followed swiftly until they came to the river's edge where they found a crowd had gathered. Coming forward, they saw the form of Elinor lying upon the grass, with several healers about her. The others stood and looked on.

Two Elves approached Malor as Shelarindel went to assist the healers. They both bowed to him. He gestured to them to speak, but his eyes were on his daughter.

"My lord Malor," began one, "we were walking along the river after breaking our fast when we heard the lady scream. We came upon her lying as she was, and a figure hooded and cloaked hung in the air above her. It turned to look at us, and then disappeared."

"It was clad in the robes of the Black Circle, my lord," added the other. Lord Malor turned to look at him.

"What? That is impossible," he said. "The Dark One was the last—"

"Malor," said Shelarindel, beckoning him. He went over to her and looked down at his daughter's face. Elinor was in some kind of stupor, her face sickly pale and holding nothing of its usual healthy glow. Her eyes were rolled back in her head, showing only the whites, and her teeth were clenched. Rivulets of sweat streaked her face.

"There are no marks of violence on her," said the healer, "No bruises or broken bones." She looked intently into Malor's eyes. "But she is with child."

The Lord of Oakdean stared at the healer in shock. How could this be? A ripple of unease went through the crowd.

"There is some kind of evil spell at work here," said Nildoron, "I can sense it."

"I too," said Malor. "This is black sorcery." The unnatural cold that had visited the scene could be felt as one could feel in an icy breeze through an open window. The sensation that magic had been done here hung in the air like the electric feeling before a storm.

"Malor," said Shelarindel, "This is a matter too great for us to deal with, let alone understand. Elinor has come under the influence of some dark and terrible spell, the likes of which I have never seen before. We must send a messenger to Algol the Bright for a representative of the Council to come and help us solve this mystery. "

"I will go for you, my lord," said Nildoron. "His Majesty wished me to speak to the Eldest after I had seen you."

Malor considered. Just this morning he had been confronted with his King's wish to not only rejoin the Elven people as a whole, but to be reconciled with his brother who had seemed to hold his position of Eldest as more important than their relationship. Now he was faced with his daughter's predicament.

"Shelarindel—" he began.

"Malor, it *must* be done." She searched his face. "This has the mark of the unspeakable powers of Malkaar."

"*Malkaar?*" Malor's whisper rasped in his throat, and he heard it repeated here and there in the crowd. The atmosphere turned suddenly chill at the mention of that name that the Elves had sought to forget over the many years since the final battle of the War of the Races.

"This cannot be. Malkaar was bound by the Ice of Foreverness." He looked to where several of the healers had brought a litter to take Elinor to the Chamber of Healing. "This must have some other explanation."

"Whatever it is," said Shelarindel, "we must have the advice of the Council." She watched his face. "Goldwen himself must be appealed to."

Malor watched the healers lift and bear his daughter away. There seemed no change in her condition. The only sounds were her ragged breathing and the steps of the healers as they progressed up the path. *My daughter*, he thought, *my only daughter*.

"If she were *my* daughter, "said Shelarindel, "I would send for him."

"Is there no other way?"

She shook her head. "Not if you hold Elinor in any regard and wish to help her." she said, holding his gaze.

It was Malor who looked away. "So be it," he said. He addressed the master of the stables who stood nearby in the crowd. "Please see that Lord Nildoron has a fresh mount."

"Yes, my lord." The stable master motioned to two of his grooms and they departed to fetch Lord Nildoron a horse.

The Lord of Oakdean turned to Nildoron. "I thank you for your offer, my lord. Are you ready to ride?"

Lord Nildoron bowed to him. "Like the wind, my lord."

Malor bowed to him in turn. Then the King's messenger left with the master of the stables. Shelarindel watched them leave, then turned to Malor, saying; "Thank you."

Malor nodded abstractedly. He then walked up the path, lost in his own thoughts. The crowd broke up, each going about their own business. Shelarindel left to go to the Chamber of Healing. In a short time the glade was empty.

Not long after, Lord Nildoron urged his mount out of the city with the message to the Council. His cloak flapped in the wind of his passage, and the riding gear of his mount jingled musically as he rode swiftly through the small villages along the Midway on his way to the city of Algol the Bright, where dwelt the greatest of wizards of Light in all Erathyn.

At midday he had ridden for three hours, and had almost closed the distance between Oakdean and Algol. The sun was hot, and twice he had stopped to drink and to spell his horse at the Silvering. Nildoron had rested for a moment, then he had mounted and rode on.

Now he sat his horse on a hill above where the city of the wizards lay. He looked down across the valley and saw the lofty spires of the many-coloured towers that made up the city. He spoke soothingly to his mount as they progressed at a walk down towards the bridge over the river that led to Algol. This was Shaped from living trees and bedecked with precious stones which glimmered as with a life of their own.

As he neared them, the towers seemed higher yet. Unlike all of the other dwellings of the Elves upon Erathyn, Algol had been Shaped from different varieties of stone. Nildoron had never been to the city before, and now his gaze roved over the marvellous achievement of that art.

He rode over the bridge and approached the main gate which was set into the centre of the wall. It was built from a white stone thirty feet high that surrounded the city. These fortifications were a reminder of the past when the War of the Races had encroached even to this peaceful area. Guards manned the main gate, although Erathyn had known no strife for many years.

Nildoron halted before the main gate. The two guards, wearing the white ceremonial armour of the Order of the Oak, with silver inlaid breastplates and helms, came to attention as they saw the torc at his throat, bringing their spears with a clash to their shoulders. Their breastplates displayed the insignia of the Order; an oak tree emblazoned in silver and gold, the sacred metals of the Elves. At their sides, they wore a sword and longknife each. Nildoron raised his hand in recognition of their salute.

"I must see the Eldest," he said. "There has been an unusual and distressing event in Oakdean, and we seek his advice and help."

"Very well, my lord," said the guard on the right. He looked up and gestured to another guard on the wall above, who disappeared from sight. A moment later, the gate opened wide, ponderously swinging on its massive hinges. The guard turned to the rider and pointed the way to the tower. "Go straight along this road and around the park. There you will find a group of towers. The second tower on your left is the Eldest's tower. The Eldest will receive you there. Enter, my lord." Both of them bowed to him.

Nildoron rode into the city. He followed the guard's instructions, and soon came to the designated tower, where he dismounted. A young boy appeared and took his horse to a stable behind the tower. The rider entered through the main door. An Elf maiden clad in the robes of a servant met him. She bowed to him.

"I am Neldriin, my lord. The Eldest waits within. Please follow me."

He followed her down a short hallway, which led to a door. The maiden opened it, and gestured for him to go through. He found himself in a small-enclosed courtyard, where a figure sat on a bench amid a lush garden. He was dressed in the long, white robe of the Council of Light, embroidered with swirling lines and characters of magic in gold, as befitted his Name of Power. His hair hung unbound almost to his waist, snowier than his robe. His face was stern to look upon; it was not in any way severe, but it was the face of someone who always did what was right, no matter what the cost. His eyes held the hint of untold knowledge and the fire of greater things. These eyes now locked on the messenger with electric focus.

"You come from Oakendean." This was a statement, not a question.

"Yes, Eldest," said Lord Nildoron. "Then you already know what has happened there today?"

"No. But I felt the stirrings of forbidden magic this day, and it was as though I had felt them before. I sensed that something was amiss in Oakendean. Please tell me what has happened." He motioned to the messenger to continue.

Nildoron then quickly told him of the events in Oakdean. The wizard sat there listening intently. When he heard Elinor's name and the condition that she was in, a shadow passed over his face. Then he rose from his seat, and the messenger had for a moment the sense of great power held in check.

"This is no ordinary spell," said the Eldest. "I believe Dark Magic is involved."

"That is what Lord Malor and Shelarindel the healer think as well, Eldest."

A slight smile hovered on Goldwen's lips, and then faded. He remembered the face of a beautiful Elf maiden, streaked with tears as he told her of his decision to join the Council. That maiden had been Shelarindel.

"Eldest?"

Goldwen came back from his thoughts with a start. "Your pardon," he said. "How was the Lady Elinor when you left?"

"It was unnatural. The child seemed to grow within her even as I looked upon her. Lady Shelarindel and the other healers were uncertain what to do. She was in some kind of trance, and would not wake."

The Eldest nodded. He picked up a small golden bell, which he rang vigorously. The boy that had taken the rider's horse entered and bowed.

"Ari," said Goldwen, "Please ready my horse, and ask Neldriin to come to me."

"At once, Eldest." The boy bowed to both of them, and then left to carry out Goldwen's command.

"You must be spent after your ride," said Goldwen. "I shall go to Oakendean alone, without any escort or retinue, as I believe that this incident will have dire consequences for all of Erathyn if I do not hasten."

"There is something else, Eldest," Nildoron said.

"Yes?"

The Elf-lord reached into the pouch at his side, and produced a scroll. He handed it to Goldwen, who unrolled it and began to read.

The Eldest met Nildoron's eye. "You know of the matter that is contained within this scroll?"

"Yes, Eldest. His Majesty intends us to return to Glindarion, and wishes Lord Malor and all of the folk of Oakdean to join us. He asked me to inform Lord Malor that is also his wish that you and Lord Malor be reconciled."

"I see," Goldwen said, rolling up the scroll. "And what was Lord Malor's response?" He handed the scroll back.

Nildoron placed it in his pouch. "He was – *reluctant*, Eldest."

Goldwen smiled. "Yes, I imagine he would have been."

The servant girl entered and bowed to them.

"Neldriin," said the wizard, "please take this guest and see that he eats and rests. He may stay here until I return. We will speak of the King's message then, my lord."

The maiden bowed again, saying; "Yes, Eldest."

"Thank you, Eldest," said Lord Nildoron. He bowed and followed the maiden.

Goldwen turned and looked at the sky, which was a light blue. A few puffs of white cloud floated here and there. It was warm and sunny, although the early afternoon sun had begun to dip towards the horizon. The birds sang joyfully, and a slight breeze stirred the trees in the garden.

The wizard was oblivious to his surroundings. He was lost in the memories of the War of the Races, and of his part in that struggle. He remembered the battles in which he had been involved, and the fallen friends and foes he had known. He seemed to hear the clash of swords, and the cries and sounds of strife. Images of magical combat came to his mind, and a twinge of pain tingled in his back, a legacy from the Last Battle which he had borne ever since.

"So, Malkaar," he said. "Somehow you have escaped your icy prison. It seems Shaarla's spell did not hold you. This time there will be an end to your evil." His face set in a mask of determination as he whirled and strode out of the garden purposefully.

Goldwen rode out of the stable and around the park. The guards at the gate brought their spears to a salute as he passed. He held his staff aloft in reply. He rode across the bridge, and then coaxed his horse into a gallop. His long white hair streamed out behind him, and his cloak flapped like wings as he passed out of sight. Behind him, Algol was painted with the rays of the setting sun.

His steed lunged forward beneath him, flashing through the villages in the dusk that Lord Nildoron had passed through in the day. As they rode like the wind, Goldwen's voice was muttering a Spell of Endurance for his mount. He would be able to ride at a greater pace than the messenger had, although his horse would be spent when they arrived. Part of his own strength was fed to his steed in this spell. The sun fell below the horizon, turning the sky red. As the light faded, Goldwen's staff glowed brightly, lighting his way like a great firefly as he rode.

His mind wandered as they sped along the road. How would Malor receive him? He had not seen his brother for many years, and Malor had been resentful and defensive when they had parted. He had never forgiven Goldwen for leaving to become a member of the Council of Light, and when he had heard that Goldwen was the Eldest, he had not spoken or sent word to him at all.

Seeing Shelarindel too, would be bittersweet. It had taken her a long time to be resigned to the fact that he was dedicated to the Council and could not return her love. Indeed, he thought that was the main reason why she had given herself wholly to the healer's craft.

Elinor he could remember as a small precocious child; she was precious to Malor, he knew. She was a living reminder of her mother who had perished in the War. He had lavished affection on her. The evil that had befallen her was a terrible thing, and he would do his utmost to help her.

The miles fell beneath the flashing hooves, and they soon came within sight of Oakdean. Goldwen allowed his mount to slow to a walk as they approached the main gate. Evening was falling, and dark clouds were gathering on the horizon. A cold wind had sprung up from out of the North, hissing in the trees as they bent in its passage. The low mutter of thunder could be heard in the distance.

As Goldwen entered the gate, he saw before him Lord Malor, who stood waiting expectantly. A group of Elves waited with him. He stopped his horse and dismounted, and several grooms came forward to take his mount. Light from torches flickered and swayed in the wind, casting shadows that danced on their faces. Lightning flashed as the storm grew nearer.

Goldwen strode forward to meet his brother. Malor bowed, and then straightened. The wizard grasped Malor on the shoulder in a greeting of the ways of Men. The Lord of Oakdean's shoulders were stiff and submissive beneath his touch. The smile on Goldwen's face faded as he sensed the other's discomfort. He let his hand fall as he heard his horse being led away. The only sounds were the hooves on the flagstones, and the dry rustling of leaves as they skittered in the rising wind. Again the lightning lit the courtyard, and the thunder rolled, louder than before.

Lord Malor finally spoke. "Welcome, Eldest." His tone was very formal. He stood before Goldwen uncomfortably. Now that the moment had come, he did not know what to say to the wizard. He recalled all of the angry words and arguments of the past, and then the long silence as he had ignored all of Goldwen's messages.

"Greetings, my lord," replied the wizard. Seeing Malor's reserve, he decided to act strictly according to custom. "I have come to help you. How is the Lady Elinor?"

"She is still in the trance, and is almost full term. Can you do anything against this sorcery?"

"We shall see. Take me to her."

Lord Malor gestured for him to follow. They walked towards the main hall, with the others bearing the guttering torches behind them. As they went, Goldwen moved closer to Malor and spoke softly in his ear.

"I know that this is awkward for you. It is just as hard for me also. His Majesty wanted me to speak to you about rejoining our people, for the time is coming when we will return to Glindarion."

Lord Malor walked along silently. Goldwen's staff stumped along on the flagstones as they proceeded. The storm approached with greater speed, and the lightning and thunder came more frequently.

"Have you nothing to say? I would think that you would welcome the opportunity to leave this world to Men and return home."

"I will follow His Majesty's commands," said Malor. "Men will do with this world what they will. They have no great love for us. They fear us, and blame us for the magic which the Dark One unleashed upon them in the war."

"And yet many of them gave their lives to defeat him. They fought alongside us and the Dwarves in the Union of Races."

"I have not forgotten," said Malor, "And I have not forgotten that many of them allied themselves with him. The Black Circle was made up of Men."

"The Black Circle was broken and destroyed," said Goldwen. "Those Men who had joined Malkaar were well repaid for their foolishness. Indeed, he used them for his own ends, sacrificing them to save himself."

"It was only what they deserved," said Malor.

They had entered the greeting hall and were making their way along the corridor to the Chamber of Healing. They met no one. The air was tense with expectancy; as though the very walls knew that something unusual was occurring.

They ascended a long flight of stairs and came to their destination. Here their escort remained as they entered the chamber. The figures inside were outlined in a flare of lighting that suddenly came through the windows.

They crossed the floor to where Elinor lay; her swollen belly a sign of strange and unknowable portent. Around her several healers were gathered. The Lady Shelarindel turned as Malor and Goldwen approached. She bowed to the wizard, saying; "Eldest. Be welcome."

Goldwen looked into her face. Time had not dealt with her unkindly. Indeed, her features were much the same as he remembered, for age did not trouble the Elves as it does the race of Man. Only a few lines of care had been written there.

"Shelarindel. It is good to see you again. I wish it were under other circumstances."

He patted her shoulder reassuringly, and then went over to the pallet on which the girl lay, sweating and breathing harshly. He could feel the aura of Darkness that surrounded her, almost palpably encroaching on the atmosphere in the chamber. He raised his staff and concentrated on his Self within. This was definitely Malkaar's doing. He could feel that now, and he shuddered as he recalled the strength of his old adversary. He recited the spell to himself inaudibly, and felt the stirrings of magic as his Self awoke. The others in the chamber became silent. The storm came closer, grumbling and booming. Only the fitful glares from outside made any movement, making shadows dance grotesquely upon the walls.

The Self separated from his body like smoke rising, and sank into the girl's body. It slipped down beneath Elinor's skin, sensing the Darkness below. It felt the skin and surface tissue give way before it as the water gives way before the plunge of a diver. Muscle, sinew and bone were penetrated in their turn, in an ever-shifting pattern of the enclosed universe of the flesh.

The sounds in the chamber were cut off abruptly in the Self's awareness as though it had plunged into a deep pool. The beat of the maiden's heart could be perceived by it like the tolling of a great bell. Around the Self, everything was bathed in the red light of her body's tissues. The flow of the girl's blood rushed by like a great river. Goldwen's Self was enveloped in the heat of Elinor's body as it travelled, and the working of the heart was becoming louder every moment. It sensed the emanations of the evil as a bitterly cold knot, which was draining the life and heat from the girl's form. The Self headed towards it. A more rapidly beating heart could be sensed, which beat in counter-point to Elinor's own.

The Self approached the focus of the evil, and recoiled at the sense of Dark Magic. The baby was fully formed and ready to be born. The Self of Goldwen gathered great forces, and as his body above strained in the task, applied them to the baby. The contending powers of Darkness and Light commenced a tremendous struggle within Elinor's body; one which was seen only dimly in the sweating girl and the straining, shivering body of Goldwen.

Suddenly, there came to the Self a vision of the Dark One seated in his tower. He was looking down, and his cowl concealed his face. He looked up, and threw the cowl back. Malkaar's ancient visage was revealed, and his evil eyes burned into Goldwen's Self. Above, the body of Goldwen cried out, and Shelarindel made to rush to its aid, but Malor held her fast, shaking his head. Goldwen's body saw a rapid montage of the Last Battle, and the pain in his back flared anew. He saw again the fall of the mountainside that had nearly killed him all those years ago.

The deadly fire in the Dark One's eyes pierced the Self as it attempted to destroy the baby. Malkaar clenched his left hand into a fist before the Self's gaze. Circling the wrist was a bracelet of silver in the shape of a snake coiled around the sorcerer's arm. In the eyes were housed oval stones as black as the Void. Impossibly, the serpent's metallic head reared up and hissed and bared its fangs at the Self. The eyes lit up with a baleful fire. A shield of Darkness encompassed the child, and against this, the Self pushed. Laughter came from the sorcerer's image as he saw that Goldwen's Self was blocked in its spell casting.

Goldwen's body shivered and swayed as though in the grasp of a gale. The pain in his back rose in intensity, until it was like a dagger of torment. Sweat ran down his face as the conflict continued. Dimly he realised that he could not defeat the Dark One in this manner. Making his decision, he changed his attack.

The Self focussed all of its power into a needle of force, and send it spearing into the shield. The Darkness was ripped open, a ray of blinding light poured in, and the baby was rent by the magic and with a stunning flash became two babies. The power of Light flowed into the second, while the first sucked the powers of Darkness into itself as though it was feeding. A cry of rage exploded from the sorcerer. The Self could do no more, and sensing that its body was stretched to the absolute limit, fled back the way it had come. Goldwen's body staggered and almost fell as his Self returned to it. His staff slipped from his hand and clattered to the floor. Both Malor and Shelarindel supported Goldwen and led him to a nearby pallet. The cries and gasps of Elinor giving birth faded in his ears as he passed out.

Goldwen regained consciousness a little while later to find Shelarindel wiping his brow. Malor stood nearby, looking between Goldwen's pallet and that of Elinor's. His gaze then moved to two small pallets from which the cries of the babies came without cease. The Eldest raised himself to a sitting position. "*Wine,*" he whispered. "*I am spent.*" His voice was weak and sibilant.

A healer brought over a goblet of wine, which Goldwen drained in one long draught. He nodded his thanks to him, and the healer took the goblet and returned to his companions who attended Elinor and her two offspring. Malor came to his side and gripped his shoulder, staring deeply into his eyes. "You were not able to destroy it," he said. "What has happened?"

The wizard felt a small glow of satisfaction at his brother's gesture of concern. He grasped his arm firmly, and managed a weak smile when Malor did not flinch at his touch.

Goldwen looked at his brother wearily. The effort of sending his Self and then of the magic cast to break through the shield had weakened him severely. "No," he replied. "There was no way to destroy it without harming your daughter. This was no ordinary spell that I faced here, it was the work of the greatest sorcerer who has ever lived, and he has somehow broken free of his eternal prison. I had a vision of him as my Self cast the counter-spell."

At this, the others in the chamber felt their blood run cold, confirming the suspicions of all as to the origins of the terrible spell. "It was not possible to allow this child to be born without some protection for our part, so I was able to affect a change, creating two such creatures and to infuse one of them with a great deal of my power. This was the only way that we could face the power of the Child of Darkness, by creating a Child of Light to fight for us and protect all Erathyn. Even I could not have hoped to defeat the Dark One's evil creation by myself."

He released Malor's arm and lay back, Shelarindel helping him to attain a small degree of comfort on the bare pallet. He realised that after this, Erathyn would never be the same, and if his plans went badly, it would not be able to withstand Malkaar's evil a second time, helped as he would be by the offspring he had created by his sorcery.

Shelarindel leaned over him and said: "So, Eldest, this other child has been created by you? Are you certain that he will help us? Will he not also be as dangerous as his twin?" Her gaze was a mixture of curiosity and anxiety. He wondered why she would feel this way, and then remembered the love that she had felt for him. That love he had forsaken for his arts.

"Be not afraid, Shelarindel," he said. "The one boy is as good as the other is evil, and I have imbued him with as much of my power as I could."

The look of trepidation on her face faded. "Then we shall cherish him as if he were your own son." She smiled and he grasped her hand.

"How is Elinor?" he asked, attempting to rise again to see. Shelarindel firmly took him by his shoulders and forced him to lie back. He was surprised at the strength in her, but did not resist.

"She sleeps," said Malor. "The births exhausted her, but she seems to be resting peacefully." He bowed to Goldwen humbly. "I thank you for your help - Eldest."

Goldwen saw that he was attempting to thank him without actually forgetting the reserve he had displayed before. It would take a long time before they would be reconciled. *Still*, he mused; *my brother does have a chink in his armour.* He accepted Malor's thanks gratefully, and smiled at his little victory.

The two babies had not stopped crying. They lay wrapped in blankets and were bawling as though they were outraged at their unnatural births. Outside, the lightning flashed and the thunder rolled and grumbled, making the windows rattle as it stalked through the night like a great hunting beast. The wind howled mournfully through the city. The storm broke, and the rain fell heavily, beating against the windows and drumming on the roof like the hooves of a hundred horses. As Goldwen heard the rain, he thought that it was only the harbinger of the terrible storm of Dark Magic to come.

The Darkness had returned.

CHAPTER II

THE COUNCIL OF LIGHT

Goldwen lay awake, thinking over the events of the day. He knew without doubt that his powers had been weakened considerably by his efforts, and that now he should consider his options. His life had been a long struggle to obtain the position of Eldest. This he had succeeded in doing, but at great cost.

The air in the chamber seemed to thicken perceptibly, as an invading energy stealthily grew in the room, unnoticed by the wizard.

"Perhaps I should step down," whispered the thought from somewhere. Goldwen pondered this thought. In his weary state, he did not sense the unseen presence in the chamber. The force of a powerful will beat upon his mind insinuatingly.

What of the Council? He had served faithfully. It had been his life's work.

"The Council will choose another leader," continued the thought.

Yes, Amberon surely. He had wanted the position for many years, chafing in his place as second to Goldwen.

"The Child of Light will need guidance," whispered the Voice.

Indeed. And I will be the one to give it. Having made his decision and finished his inner debate, the wizard then slipped into a peaceful sleep. A sensation of satisfaction seemed to hang in the air, and then the artful power faded away.

In his chamber, the Lord of Oakdean worried about his daughter. She had been given a sleeping draught, and Shelarindel had assured him that she would sleep soundly. He did not forget that the last time they had spoken, he had been angry with her and he had sent her away. Now, he wished that he had not dismissed her. In one sense, Elinor was right. There were good peoples in all the races of Erathyn. It was just that he had not liked to be seen arguing with her in front of Lord Nildoron. Finally, worn out with his concern, he slept.

Oakdean awoke to a dull, grey dawn. A vast mass of swollen clouds had rolled down from the North, bringing with them the threat of rain. The sun was only a dim, pale disc, glimpsed from time to time in the gloom. A light drizzle fell, and all was quiet and still. None stirred in the city, except for the grooms as they made the horses ready for the journey to Algol the Bright. A wagon with two horses had been provided for the two babies, for the Eldest had decided that they would be taken to the city of the wizards. Here they would be shown to the Council of Light. A messenger had been dispatched to summon the Council to meet in two days.

Goldwen, Shelarindel, and Malor sat breaking their fast in the banqueting hall. The gloom from outside seemed to pervade the hall and wrap each of them in their own thoughts. Even the fire in the hearth seemed drained of its usual cheery warmth.

"A great evil has returned to Erathyn," said Goldwen. "I must return to Algol. Many decisions must be made about these children, and also for the actions of the Council." His face was grim as he spoke; the gravity of the situation was reflected in his every move and glance. Malor leaned forward as if he would speak, and then changed his mind. He sat back in his chair and was silent.

"Eldest," said Shelarindel, "what is to be done with these children?"

Goldwen looked deeply into her eyes, and she could see that his powers had indeed waned since he had sent his Self into Elinor's body.

"I shall discuss that with the Council," he replied. He looked at Malor, who turned away and gazed into the fire. No music was heard this morning; only an uncomfortable silence reigned as they ate. The others in the hall did not speak, sensing their mood. The only sound was of the utensils of the diners, and the muted crackling of the ineffectual fire. None commented on the unusual coldness in Spring, although all there felt it.

The group left Oakdean an hour later and headed towards Algol. The light rain had ceased, but the sky was still dark and overcast. Two of the grooms travelled with them for the care of the horses. The Lord of Oakdean had left the city in the hands of one of his lords. He went with the party mainly because he was concerned for his daughter. In the morning, she had not spoken, and had not reacted to anyone's presence, staring blankly. Shelarindel and the other healers were at a loss.

Goldwen and Malor rode side by side just ahead of the wagon, which contained, apart from the children, Shelarindel and Lindsa, one of her assistants. The Elf maiden Elinor seemed to be wasting away as they rode, even as her children seemed to grow at an unnatural pace. They were also strangely silent. The Child of Light was fair to look upon, with blond hair and large blue eyes, which seemed to take everything in. He smiled at Shelarindel and Lindsa in the cool shade of the wagon. The Child of Darkness, however, had a malicious look, with eyes as black as a midnight sky bereft of stars. His hair was also black. Both children had an air of preternatural intelligence, which was unnerving to see in such young faces. The innocence normal in a child's gaze was not present in either of them. The children grew almost as they watched, and poor Elinor moaned from time to time, with sweat running down her once youthful face, ageing before their very eyes. Occasionally, Lord Malor would look back over his shoulder at the wagon.

The company continued towards Algol. They rode at a comfortable pace, and a light breeze was cool on their faces. The horse's hooves set up a clopping on the stones of the road, leather saddles creaked, and harness jingled peacefully as they went on their way. The wagon wheels rolled upon the road in an endless rumble.

At about mid-day, Goldwen called a halt for a rest and food by a swift running stream that was a tributary of the Silvering. Malor looked in the wagon at his daughter. She had fallen into a restless sleep, and Shelarindel and Lindsa took turns to mop her sweating face. He was worried that she had not regained her wits. As the others made themselves comfortable, the wizard motioned to his brother to join him, and they went and sat a little way apart. The stream flowed musically past them, and the breeze whispered and sighed amongst some old willows that were standing near. Birds could be heard singing and calling around them. The two grooms unhitched the horses and led them and the other mounts to the stream to drink.

"Well," said Malor, "Are you certain that this is the doing of your old enemy?"

Goldwen nodded grimly. "The signs are his," he said, stroking his chin. "I do not know what this means, but somehow his evil has returned to trouble us." Goldwen's eyes narrowed, and his face was set in hard lines. Malor had turned to look at the stream.

"I must step down as Eldest," said Goldwen suddenly.

Malor spun around, his face registering his shock. "What?" He looked as if he had been struck in the heart. The group over near the wagon looked up in surprise at his shout. He noticed their alarm and signed with a wave of his hand that all was well. He turned back to his brother, and for the first time saw the other's great weariness.

"But you have been Eldest for many years. It was the only thing that you ever wished to be," Malor said. "This is unbelievable."

Goldwen nodded. "I know of your disgust with my involvement with the Council, and of your loathing of our magic, because it is of a more involved and dangerous kind than that of Shaping and Healing." He grasped Malor's arm, and drew him closer. "This is a thing that is much more important than you realise, brother," he said. "It is far more important than my position at Algol, even more important than the Council itself."

Malor was astonished. He had never heard Goldwen speak in this manner before. His brother's life had been one of total dedication to the Council of Light. He had forsaken everything for it, including his love for Shelarindel.

"If Malkaar is not destroyed this time, the world will fall into a great darkness, from which there will be no hope of ever regaining peace for its entire folk," said Goldwen. "I tell you this because I will have great need of you."

He released Malor's arm, and held out his hand. "I know it is much to ask," he said.

Malor looked at his brother's hand, and thought of all the times that his friendship had been overlooked for Goldwen's obsession with the Council, and of his unrelenting drive to rise to its head. He remembered when his brother had told them of his decision to leave them, and he had had to comfort Shelarindel, to hold her, to soothe her with words that he did not really mean. He loved the healer himself, although she had never returned that love. Because he was honourable, he had never told Shelarindel of these feelings, knowing that she wept for his undeserving brother. He recalled all of the lonely days and nights he had passed as the Lord of Oakdean since his wife had died, trying to see his position as some kind of compensation for his brother's dedication and his own unrequited love for Shelarindel.

He looked at Goldwen's outstretched hand with resentment. But as he saw the pleading in the other's eyes, he remembered that it was Goldwen who had organized the fight against Malkaar, and he recalled his brother's great struggle with the enemy of Erathyn. In that moment, he realised that whatever he and the folk of Oakdean thought, if it were not for his brother's devotion to his arts, all would have been lost. He held out his hand, and the two gripped each other firmly. Goldwen's face showed his relief.

Then the group gathered themselves together after their rest by the stream and rode on. Around sunset they approached Algol. The great wall was like a line of fire in the dying light of the sun. The towers glittered, giving off shards of light, and were all washed in the red glow of the sunset. Malor stared at the blood-red towers, and was filled with foreboding. He seemed to see a vision of fire and slaughter; the towers burned, and fell. He passed his hand across his eyes, and the vision faded.

They rode across the bridge and came to the gate, where two guards saluted them.

"Has the Council been summoned?" asked Goldwen.

"Yes, Eldest," replied one of the guards. "It will meet tomorrow as you instructed."

The wizard nodded in response, and then he led the group into the city. The others looked about themselves. They had never been to Algol, and in the towers of Shaped stone that met their gaze; their

King's power was evident. They rode around the park and came to the Eldest's tower. Here Lord Nildoron, who waited with Ari, greeted them. The boy came forward to assist the grooms with the horses. Lord Nildoron stepped out smiling to greet them, but the smile fell as he saw their serious faces.

"How is the Lady Elinor?" He asked.

"She has had two children," said Goldwen, "but she is not herself."

He showed with a nod of his head the two children, who stood silently by the group. Nildoron was astonished. He had expected to see two babies, not these boys before him. Here was certain proof of the effects of the Dark Magic.

They turned to see Shelarindel and Lindsa lifting the silent form of Elinor on a litter down from the wagon. Lord Malor hovered over his daughter, tears shining in his eyes. The wizard motioned to them to bring her inside the tower, and the group followed him and the two healers and their burden within. Here he left Nildoron with the two children in the dining chamber. He led the others to a small chamber, which opened onto the garden in the courtyard. They lifted the slight form onto a bed. Lord Malor came forward and stroked his daughter's face. She moaned and stirred, but made no sign of waking. The pallor of her face was unnatural in the candlelight, and her once fine features were gaunt. Shelarindel put a hand on his shoulder.

"We have done all we can for her," she said gently. "Let her rest, my lord. Lindsa and I will watch by her side tonight."

He bowed, thanking them. No words came from his lips. Goldwen led him from the room and into the dining chamber, where the others waited.

The Elf maiden Neldriin appeared at the summons of Goldwen and provided them with food and drink. They all ate silently, casting glances at the two children from time to time. An atmosphere of tense waiting filled the room. After the group had eaten and drunk their fill, they all retired to rooms that were provided for their comfort. So the night passed away. The candle in the window where the two healers watched in turns by the wasted figure of Elinor was the only light.

The morning came with rays of brilliant sunshine. The gloom of the previous day had been swept away, but all hearts there were heavy as they thought of Elinor's state, and they wondered how the Council would react to the children's presence. Goldwen and his party, Malor, Shelarindel, Lindsa, Nildoron, and the two children left the Tower of the Eldest. Two servants bore the litter upon which Elinor lay. The two children grew almost as one looked upon them, even as the once beautiful and young Elf maiden who bore them wasted away, as if her vitality were being drained from her and fed to them. The whole group made their way to the meeting place of the Council, the Tower of Cherrdelion.

The tower itself stood in the centre of the City of the Wizards, and as the most important building, was the largest there. It had been crafted by the great arts that had been studied and handed down through many ages. The stone of its construction was called *scarlite*; beautiful to see, being primarily of a rosy hue with blood-red veins that ran through it. It soared fully one hundred feet high, standing tall above all of the other towers, as befitted its station. At the very top lay a great landing; this was wrought of stone and living wood, and was decorated with many jewels that sparkled in the sun. Pennants flapped in the wind high above the ground, one to each corner. Five sided the tower was, to represent the Primal Elements; Earth, Air, Fire, Water, Void, and it had five doors also; the North door being the largest and the main entrance.

It was a huge oval portal with a door thrice the height of the tallest Elf, made of wood lovingly Shaped by the magic of the Elves. Upon it shone the symbols of the Council; a circle of six eight-pointed stars, three to a side, with a seventh, much larger than the others, in the centre of the circle. These were cunningly fashioned from gold and silver; the smaller stars were silver, and the central one was gold. This door opened ponderously to admit Goldwen and his party. On either side stood two guards that clashed spear to breastplate as the Eldest entered.

They climbed a long flight of steps, wide enough to admit three Elves walking abreast. The walls were all bedecked with tapestries depicting scenes from the history of the city, and all but Goldwen gazed around the huge hall that they were entering. This was in the form of a circle, located at the very heart of the tower. Beautiful windows of multi-coloured glass let in the light of the sun, and created prismatic rainbows of colour on the floor. Directly above was a huge skylight set in the ceiling that also contributed to the ethereal glow of the hall. Against the far wall upon a raised platform was the table of the Council, before rows of seats that faced it from the floor.

Within were the other members of the Council. They were six in number, Goldwen as Eldest made up their number to seven. Seven to the Elves was a Number of Power. They were ranged about the semi-circular table, and its ends were open to the gallery, so that whomever they were speaking to could face them all at the same time.

These were their names and their arrangement: Firstly, on the far right of the table, was Narwen, Master of Earth magic. He was a tall blonde Elf who usually said little at such proceedings. Then next to him was Vandaron, the Master of Birds, who could converse with all manner of them. He had the look of some proud eagle, with his brown hair, and clear, piercing blue eyes. Then there was Korwen, Master of Air magic. He was a silent, strong looking individual with dark hair and eyes. The seat next to Korwen in the middle of the table was that of the Eldest. Then on the other side was Amberon, Master of Water magic; second in power and knowledge to Goldwen himself. He had dark brown hair and wore a detached expression on his face. Then Vairon, the Master of Beasts, who looked himself like a great bear, who was of a more solid build than the other Elves, and Telewen, Master of Fire magic. He was also the historian and the Keeper of Records, and had the placid, patient look of a librarian. They represented all of the Primal Elements of magic; Goldwen himself was the Master of Void magic. As he entered, a great gong was sounded, its earthy tones rolling through the stone itself.

Standing before them on the gallery floor was an Elf clad in grey robes and holding a ceremonial staff in his right hand. He was Candreen, the advisor to the Council. His dark hair and eyes took in the sight of the approaching group, and his eyes narrowed as the two children became clear to his gaze. He turned slightly and glanced sidelong at Amberon, who was his real master. A quizzical look crossed Amberon's face, and then he motioned Candreen to carry out his duties with a warning look. Candreen turned and waited.

Candreen's staff struck the floor, once. "All hail the Eldest!" he cried.

All of the Council rose to their feet. "Hail, Eldest!" they cried with one voice. Goldwen raised his hand in acknowledgment. The Councillors bowed to Goldwen as he strode forward and took his seat, and then they sat in their places.

The Councillors white robes were chased with the characters and symbols of their special magical skills, the lapel designs showing the colours associated with their magic, Earth; brown, Air; light blue, Fire; orange, Water; dark blue, and the Void shown on Goldwen's robes, black. The lapels of Vandaron's robe depicted feathers of many kinds, and that of Vairon's showed all kinds of pelts and skins. They all wore belts of red except for Goldwen, whose white belt denoted his higher status.

Before the table, facing its centre was the gallery with rows of wooden seats, which showed the cunning work of Shaping. The others that had entered with Goldwen seated themselves there. The roof of the hall stretched away into heights that were filled with dark wooden rafters. The walls gave off a lambent glow where there were torches in tall sconces flickering. Goldwen stood and addressed the Council.

"Brothers," he began, "We are met for the purpose of deciding what our part should be in this grave matter that has come upon us. It seems clear to me now that our age-old adversary has somehow broken the spell that bound him, and has escaped his icy prison. He has also reached out and touched our folk with an evil that must be answered." His eyes sought each of them in turn.

The Councillors looked at the two children and the emaciated form on the litter. They could feel the emanations of Dark Magic that radiated from them. The Child of Light looked all around the hall, curiosity written on his face as each new thing met his eye. The Child of Darkness stood aloof, his brazen stare a challenge to the Council. Elinor lay breathing shallowly, as Shelarindel hovered over her in concern, and Malor stood near and watched. It was plain to all that her condition was a violation against nature, and an abomination in the sight of the Elves, who venerated the mother of all things.

An unseen presence invaded the room. Energy inimical to the Elves gathered itself above the dais, as though it listened to their converse. Only one Elf, Telewen, frowned to himself and looked around the hall, seeming to feel its presence.

It floated down to hover by Candreen's side.

"This cannot be Malkaar's doing," whispered the Voice in his head.

"This cannot be Malkaar's doing," Candreen echoed.

Goldwen looked at the advisor warily. He knew that Candreen was Amberon's tool. But he would not allow him to upset this meeting. "It is not your place to speak, Candreen."

"But I only serve the Council...," offered the cold tones.

"But I only serve the Council . . . and you, Eldest." He bowed low. As he straightened, his gaze swept the table. "I only wish to assist you. Surely that is why I am advisor to the Council?"

Amberon smiled to himself. It was not the first time that Candreen had goaded the Eldest. Goldwen noticed the smile, but ignored it.

Telewen scanned the room, searching for the strange power.

"We do not require your advice in this matter. The Council will decide what is to be done." Goldwen's look was stern, brooking no argument.

Candreen bowed again, this time somehow making the motion a mocking gesture.

The subtle power floated up beside Amberon.

"It is a valid point...," said the Voice in his mind.

In Amberon had long lay the desire to be the leader of the Council, and many times before, he and Goldwen had had arguments on great matters. Now, the Voice persuaded him to confront his senior.

"It is a valid point, Eldest," he said. "How could the Dark One have done this?"

Goldwen beckoned to Shelarindel and Malor. They helped Elinor to rise from her litter and came forward, bringing the wasted form with them. She stood before them. The once beautiful girl could hardly stand, and was piteous to behold. A murmur came from the table.

"Can you deny that this maiden has been the victim of sorcery?" Goldwen said. "Surely you can sense that somehow the Dark Magic of the Black Circle is to blame. Somehow Malkaar has returned and done this."

"Can there be another answer, Eldest?" Korwen asked. "Perhaps there is another who has used this forbidden knowledge. It has been almost a thousand years since the last battle. Malkaar was locked in the Ice of Foreverness. Surely it cannot be he who is responsible? How can he have broken the spell and escaped?"

Goldwen regarded him. "I do not know. But I tell you he has done this. You forget, Korwen, that of all the members of the Council, I am the only one who has faced the Dark One in single combat. I tell you the sorcery that has been used here is unmistakeably his. I am certain of it. Use your senses to see for yourself that it is indeed Malkaar who is responsible."

The Councillors bent their senses upon the unfortunate girl. Lingering about her was the unmistakeable taint of Dark Magic. Could it be true? Had Malkaar done this terrible thing?

"You are right, Eldest," Vairon said. "Surely the Dark One has done this. How, I do not know, but I agree with you. The signs are his."

"I agree also," said Vandaron. "This poor girl has been touched by the sorcery of the Black Circle."

The other Councillors admitted that Goldwen was right.

Amberon stared at the girl, his thoughts whirling. What could he say?

"You must react...They know..."

"Indeed, Eldest," Amberon said. "I can sense the black touch of Malkaar upon this poor maiden. You speak truly."

"Then we are agreed that we must face and destroy him?"

Amberon looked at Goldwen, envying him his position of power. Guile entered his heart, for he had always coveted the Eldest's place and wanted it for his own.

"But we are not strong enough," said the Voice to Amberon.

"But we are not strong enough to face him. You yourself he mastered and nearly destroyed."

A twinge of pain in Goldwen's back emphasised the words of the Master of Water magic. Goldwen ruefully recalled the times that he had confronted the Dark Magic of Malkaar, and the many defeats that the Council had suffered. The Elves had not expected a mere mortal Man to wield such power.

Amberon turned to the other members of the Council. "Who will face him?" He looked at them all in turn.

"You, Telewen?" The Elf paled. He was the least of them.

"You, Vandaron?"

Vandaron did not reply. "Korwen? Narwen? Vairon?" Nobody answered. Amberon smiled. "You see, Eldest? There must be another way."

"Indeed, Amberon, there is another way."

The entire hall was hushed. The very air seemed to still. Goldwen gestured to Lindsa. She came forward with the two children. Everyone could see the spurts of growth that their bodies made in their speedy progress. They all could feel the magic that had been used here, and could see the rapid advancement of the pair's growth. Also it was apparent that here was the evidence of Dark Magic that Goldwen's messenger had spoken of. The wizards were disturbed. Amberon began to see that this could be a situation to be turned to his advantage.

"This does not concern us, "prompted the Voice.

"This is not our concern, Eldest," he said haughtily. "We should kill them both, since we do not have the strength to face Malkaar, and we do not know why he has done this. We should be trying to discover how he could escape the Ice of Foreverness." Amberon looked at the gathering as he spoke, and saw that some there agreed with him, but others did not.

Telewen gazed at Amberon, sensing the strange energy that surrounded him. He looked around and saw that no one else seemed to feel anything amiss.

Goldwen shook his head. "I have put most of my former power into this boy, (he indicated the Child of Light) and I have an idea what Malkaar plans, but I cannot be sure. However, I do agree with you, Amberon. We must know what our enemy is about, so I say we should send some scouts to his old stronghold in the North."

"That is if it is truly his doing. Why would he create this child? Surely he would do better to create an army with which to conquer

Erathyn," said Narwen, waving a hand at the Child of Darkness. It was well known that he was a supporter of Amberon, and had long been the opponent of Goldwen.

"I believe," said the Goldwen, "that he intends to reform the Black Circle."

Both Amberon and Korwen's faces showed disbelief. The other members of the Council shifted in their seats.

The presence flowed around Korwen. It insinuated itself into his mind.

"They were destroyed..."

"But they were destroyed long ago, Eldest. Surely he is only interested in taking power for himself?" Korwen sat back in his seat, convinced of his point being taken. He didn't realise that the power had spoken through him.

Telewen turned his puzzled gaze to Korwen. What was it that he could feel?

"Do we have any proof of this?" The speaker was Vandaron. He always sided with Goldwen, and was a long and trusted friend. Goldwen smiled in recognition of his defender.

"We do not. Hence the reason why I want to send some scouts to the Dark One's old stronghold, and have them report back to us what they see."

Vandaron rose. "I will go, Eldest. An eagle is faster than any scouts, even Elven ones." He gave Goldwen a smile.

"Thank you, Vandaron. Go and investigate, and come back with your news quickly."

"As you say, Eldest." He walked to the front of the table, bowed to Goldwen, and then nodded to the Councillors. "Brothers." He strode across the floor, opened the door, and left the chamber.

"Perhaps he will find nothing," Candreen said.

Goldwen saw the look that Amberon and Candreen exchanged. He knew that they were trying to agitate him. He ignored the advisor's snide comment.

"The two witnesses who saw the apparition in Oakendean said it wore the robes of the Black Circle," he said. "I think that Malkaar has created the Child of Darkness to somehow aid him in recreating the

Circle. But we must be certain. We must know why he has done this thing."

"*Ridiculous!*" cried Amberon. "He allowed the others to be destroyed, sacrificed for his own gain! Why would he seek to form the Circle again? If it is truly he that has done this, then he would have no need of underlings." Korwen nodded in assent. Narwen caught his eye and smiled conspirationally. He also was a confederate of Amberon.

The subtle energy floated down towards Goldwen. Telewen's unease increased. There was something not right about all of this. But no one else seemed to notice anything strange. He wondered what it could be.

"That is true, Amberon," said Goldwen. "However, it is what I believe. It is a riddle, and riddles exist to be solved." Goldwen looked around the whole Council. The unseen presence surrounded him.

"*Now...*" it whispered to him.

"I do not have the power to lead you in this conflict, so I must step down as Eldest, and devote myself to the solving of this riddle."

Upon the faces of the wizards were shocked and disbelieving looks as this statement was delivered. Goldwen raised his hands above his head, and clasped them together. Amberon's eyes glittered.

"*I promised you...,*" said the Voice to him.

Goldwen's voice rolled out powerfully. "By my blood, bone, brain and heart. This Council as Eldest I now depart." He unclasped his hands and lowered them slowly to his side. "I step down as Eldest. Choose my successor. Choose wisely." Then, unwinding his belt of office, he placed it on the table before the Eldest's seat. Amberon's eyes followed his every move, and then he looked up at Goldwen amazed. Goldwen bowed before them and walked around the table and stepped down from the platform to the floor.

"*Excellent...*" Amberon heard. Telewen looked over at the Master of Water magic. Surely someone else could sense the strange presence in the hall? Then he saw the look on Amberon's face. Not only was the look of triumph there that he expected to see, but also Amberon sat motionless, as though he listened to a voice that he alone could hear.

There were gasps of astonishment all through the hall. Of all there, only Malor had known. He was still shocked. Until now he thought that his brother would not give up his position. The Council was in turmoil. They all spoke at once, which resulted in uproar. No one had stepped down in this manner for many years. It was almost unheard of that a wizard would voluntarily give up such a position of power. Especially since that wizard had had to fight his way up through the ranks as Goldwen had done.

He addressed them once more. "I will take charge of these children, and perhaps I will find a way to defeat Malkaar with his own magic."

Even as Goldwen spoke, a shrill scream came from Elinor. She fell to the floor and lay still, a shrivelled thing; death had taken her. Her vitality and life force had fled from her body and flowed into the two children. Malor fell to his knees by her side, his tears flowing freely as he held her body tightly to his chest, which was wracked with deep sobs. Shelarindel knelt and attempted to soothe him.

The two children now had the stature of young boys. The Child of Light stood dismayed, staring at the corpse of Elinor, with tears running down his face.

But the Child of Darkness grinned at everyone in terrible glee.

"It is done..." Amberon heard.

Goldwen crossed the floor to where his brother knelt, anguish written on his face. The chamber erupted into bedlam; the Council left their seats and stepped down to the floor. All save Amberon and Telewen. The Master of Fire magic stared at Amberon, who was silent and still seemed to be listening to something. Candreen glanced up from the gallery floor at Amberon, who met his eye with a smirk of satisfaction. A sly look passed between them, and then Candreen became aware of Telewen's searching gaze. Amberon followed Candreen's eyes as they warned him of the other's scrutiny. Amberon turned to Telewen, who was surprised at the fierce stare that Amberon unleashed on him.

He bowed shakily to him, then stood and hurried down to the floor. Amberon's eyes followed him. What did he suspect? Amberon turned again to Candreen, and by the way his master looked at him, Candreen knew that Amberon would deal with Telewen. He nodded in agreement.

"Remember our bargain...," Amberon heard in his mind.

Yes, the bargain. Malkaar had promised him that he would be the Eldest. He looked down at the fools surrounding the dead maiden. Soon he would be their master. He smiled to himself.

The invading force faded as the hall was filled with confused voices.

CHAPTER III

MALOR AND GOLDWEN

In the courtyard of the tower Goldwen had been given, Malor and Goldwen (no longer Eldest) sat in silence. It was early morning, and the sun was burning off a light mist as it rose and promised the start of a warm day. They could hear birdsong and the noises of the city around them. Last night, after the startling events in the Tower of Cherrdelion, Goldwen had taken what little possessions he had, surrendered the keys to the Master of Void Magic's tower, and left it to the servants of Amberon, who had been sworn in by the Council as Eldest, fulfilling his long dream at last. The Eldest's tower was always the one occupied by the wizard who held that title, regardless of which magical discipline they represented. For the moment, the position of Master of Void Magic was vacant, but Goldwen had no doubt that it would soon be filled.

Everyone in the city by now had heard of the event and in the street, many confused voices could be heard.

"What do you think this means?"

"Amberon is now the Eldest!"

"It's unbelievable. Goldwen has done something that has not been done for many years."

"What is to be done with the two children?"

These and many other astonished conversations could be heard in the city streets. Goldwen had asked that he and Malor be left alone in the courtyard until the midday hour. They had much to discuss.

The two sat on a bench with a small table before them. On it were a bottle of honey-wine, and two goblets. Goldwen listened to the birdsong and wondered how he could bring his brother out of the depression he had fallen into.

"My brother," he said. "There is much that I should explain to you, for what has happened is the most important event to occur in Erathyn for many years." He looked closely at Malor. Since the death of his beloved daughter, Malor had become silent and withdrawn. Her body had been taken away until that evening when they would honour her memory in the ceremony of farewell. Goldwen had had him taken to his tower, and since then Malor had not spoken a single word, and had only fallen into a deep sleep after he had shed many tears. The Lord of Oakdean was unresponsive and just stared blankly at the wall.

"I am quite sure that there is a great deal that you would like to know, for this event is but the latest link of a long chain of events stretching back before the War of the Races." Goldwen waited for a response, but Malor was still silent.

As he spoke, the sun broke through the mist: everything in the courtyard was flooded with a golden glow. The scene was peaceful, and the horror of last night seemed far away. As the silence lengthened between them, Goldwen wondered if his brother even knew where he was. Perhaps his mind had broken?

The uncomfortable silence was broken by a deep sigh that came from Malor, sounding as if it rose from the depths of his being. His eyes cleared and Goldwen could see the pain written on his face.

"Why?" He said. "Elinor was an innocent child. She did not deserve to die like this." He shook his head, and stared down at the ground.

"I am sorry, Malor, but now we must find out why this thing has been done," replied Goldwen. "I cared for her too. But now you must be strong."

His brother's head came up. His face was set.

"*Strong?* I will be strong, Goldwen. But for her, not for *you*. I will help you in honour of her." His fists clenched and unclenched, and now he moved restlessly on the bench. Goldwen had seen his brother's anger before. He watched and waited to see what Malor would do. Then, his anger seemed to pass; only the smouldering of his eyes remained as he fixed his gaze upon Goldwen. With an effort, Malor relaxed in his seat.

He cleared his throat and said gruffly; "Tell me of Malkaar."

Goldwen could see that he had only locked his anger deep within himself. Still, the response showed that his brother was aware, even if his grief was still raw.

"Well," began Goldwen, "In the beginning, Malkaar was a friend to all. He had learnt some magic through his own efforts. He only used it for the good of all the peoples. At one point, he approached the Council, and asked if we would teach him the secrets of our own magic. Amberon stood for him, and the Council agreed. So he was instructed in the arts of Elven magic. As you know in those days long ago, we tried to help Men and guide them. He seemed to be only interested in helping everyone . Malkaar was a good student, and appeared to be full of humility; humbling himself before the Council, as though he worshipped us. But he stole our knowledge, and twisted it for his own ends.

"He unearthed the ancient knowledge of the Black Circle, and to this he added the skills which we ourselves had given him. Still he did not appear to be a threat, persuading all with his silken voice that he was only interested in the practices of such arts in an historical sense. He left Algol and went into the wastelands of the North, where the tower of the Black Ones still stood. This he took and used for his own. And if any of the Elves warned against the danger of reawakening old evil, he scoffed and said that to understand and keep evil at bay, one must study its source.

"When I first learned that he had studied the black practices of Dark Magic from elder days, I did not think much about it, neither did the Council. If you remember, I had just come into the position of Eldest, and in my pride, I thought that one Man's clumsy efforts would not disturb us."

Malor nodded. "I remember that you were quite arrogant and very sure of yourself."

"Yes," sighed Goldwen. "I was wrong. The Council and I ignored the presence of Malkaar for too long. Even when some unwholesome tales came out of the North, still we did not stir ourselves. We were happy in our ignorance, and lived in a false peace, could we but have known it. The first really disturbing thing that moved us was the report that Malkaar had been trying his hand at Shaping, and we heard that he had Shaped terrible beast-men from the lowest specimens of Men and animals. The most terrifying of these were the Cobrans, who were Shaped from Man and snake." He paused, recalling the first tales that the Council had heard.

"Yes," said Malor, "I recall hearing some of this. Please go on."

The wizard rose and picked up the bottle of wine before him, filling a goblet. With a gesture, he invited Malor to join him. His brother shook his head irritably, and motioned for him to continue with his tale. Goldwen took a sip of wine.

"After we had heard this," he resumed, "I gathered the Council to decide what we would do. The meeting was not very satisfactory. Amberon, as usual, did not want to be involved in the affairs of Men, and I am afraid that we had quite a heated argument about it. He said that Men were best left to their own devices, as long as they did not involve us in their business. The Council was divided.

"I felt so strongly about Malkaar, that I sent several scouts to see his stronghold and report back to us. Four left. Only one returned, and he was near death. Hurriedly the Council met at the Tower of Cherrdelion to hear his words. He told of a great army gathering in the North, and of the massing of forces and war materials that were poised to strike across the Great Plain. Malkaar's scouts had slain his comrades and had pursued him all the way to the Shilmaren, and he had only just escaped them. After he had spoken his warning, the brave fellow died, for he had two of the snake-men's arrows in his back."

Malor sat and listened in silence. He had not heard of the initial encounter before, and had only a sketchy outline of how the Elves had entered the war. His simmering anger slowly ebbed as he listened to the account of the past.

"And so," said Goldwen, "The entire Vale was raised for combat, and Algol became a fortress. We found later that Malkaar's emissaries had been to many of the cities in Erathyn with his promise of a greater world to come - though only if he were its ruler. At about this time, a herald of King Erodur of Rewes rode into the city to entreat for our aid in the coming conflict, and the King and the Council met with him. We eventually decided - no thanks to Amberon - that we would send ten thousand of our bowmays, esteemed throughout Erathyn, and five thousand of our riders to Erodur's aid. Most of them died in the Battle of the Great Plain. It was our darkest hour. Many of our people, including Amberon, were incensed at their loss and loud in their protest at our involvement in the affairs of Men, even though we had triumphed."

Malor nodded. "Yes, it is true. We were victorious, but our losses were great. I was with Erodur when he fell. Many of our people died in the battle. Almost all of the forces that were committed to battle by Anarys were slain, and many others were badly wounded. Even though we had defeated the enemy, so many of our own had fallen, that it was a hollow victory." He paused, remembering the carnage of that day long ago. "My wife fell also. I had tried to make her stay behind; safe, and far away from the conflict, but she was adamant in her wish to join us for the fight."

Malor's eyes took on a far away look, and he sat silently for a moment. Finally he continued, his voice soft, so that Goldwen had to lean forward to hear him speak.

"She rode into the thick of the battle, her sword laying waste amongst the enemy. She fought like a woman possessed. Her escort were hard put to keep up with her. I was with Erodur and my own warriors, and we were advancing, pushing the Dark One's rabble before us. Their battle line had collapsed, thanks to the combined strength of our horse, and the Avianinn above us, who sent arrow after arrow into their ranks. The Dwarves also made their presence felt. They are almost unstoppable once they begin to push forward with their axes." He took up his goblet and drank deeply until it was empty. Goldwen reached out, picked up the bottle, and refilled his goblet.

Malor went on: "We knew we were winning. Malkaar's army was no match for us. We did not know that he had committed most of his forces to face Anarys, but it was plain to us that his warriors were losing. Victory was in our grasp; thousands of his warriors had fallen, the ranks before us were crumbling, we could sense that the tide was turning. The Army of Darkness was about to suffer its death blow; crushed and broken by our army as we pressed our attack." He stopped speaking and stared at the table top.

The wizard watched him closely, and waited for him to go on. He knew that Malor was thinking of his wife's death, so he allowed him to take his time. They had never spoken of it before, and Goldwen knew how much anger and grief still festered in Malor's heart. There was anger there, not only against him, but for Anarys also. Finally, Malor looked up and met Goldwen's eye.

"Then - " he began. His voice faltered. Tears welled up in his eyes. He cleared his throat.

"Then we saw Elloriin and her escort swallowed by a rush of the Dark One's warriors. They surged forward in a final attempt to turn us aside. The mounted warriors were struck down, their horses screaming as they were speared. The riders were flung to the ground, and immediately they were surrounded by the enemy, and were fighting for their lives. I made to go to her aid, but at that very moment, the wave of the Cobrans attacked us. I fought savagely, knowing that Elloriin was in desperate peril, but there seemed to be a score of the hated snake-men between us. One of them slew Erodur, and most of my escort fell also. I slashed and hacked with my sword in a nightmare of fangs and black blood. Suddenly, as often happens on a battlefield, the enemy vanished, save for the corpses that lay in the mud. I rushed over to where I had seen Elloriin and her escort, but it was too late. There she lay, broken and bloody amongst the dead, her armour rent and pierced. I leapt down from my horse as the remnants of my escort arrived, and fell to my knees at her side. She gazed at the sky with sightless eyes. I took her in my arms, and crushed her cold form to my breast." Again he ceased to speak, choked with memory and emotion. The tears that had welled up in his eyes flowed down his face.

Golwen longed to reach out and comfort him, but he didn't know if Malor would reject his sympathy. So he sat and averted his gaze, while Malor wept.

"After that," Malor eventually said, his voice husky, "I ordered six of my warriors to take my lady away from the battle line. I mounted my horse, and rejoined the fray. I was filled with a cold rage; none could stand before my fury. I slew anyone who was foolhardy enough to face me. I do not remember much of the rest of the battle. I know that my warriors protected me, for I fought with no sense of self preservation. I should have been slain myself many times, but they remained at my side, and kept me from harm. Eventually, it was over. The Dark One's army had ceased to exist; utterly destroyed, their black corpses covered the Great Plain like thousands of dead black ants."

Malor took another drink. "The rest you know. Losing Elloriin was such a terrible blow to me. I was angry with Anarys for allowing her to die. I blamed him; I blamed you, for you had advised him to march against Malkaar, and in that way you shared the blame for her death. I wanted nothing more to do with you both, or the Elven world." He lapsed into silence, his face cold.

"So you took your people and separated yourselves from not only the Elven world, but from all of Erathyn." Goldwen rose to his feet, and walked over to the garden. He reached out and took hold of a dead branch. With a sharp wrench, he snapped it off and turned to regard Malor. "This branch is dead. It has ceased to be a functioning part of the tree, so I removed it. This does not mean that I should uproot the tree because one branch is dead."

"Spare me your philosophy, Goldwen," Malor said bitterly. "The decision to distance my people from the strife that Men had brought about was mine and mine alone. If you and Anarys had not involved us in it, Elloriin would still be alive."

The wizard shook his head. "No, Malor. If we had not been involved, the other races would not have been able to stand against the Dark One's army. If we had stood idly by while he carried out his dream of world domination, sooner or later, he would have crushed them all, and then he would have sent his forces against us. You cannot blame the King for her death. You allowed her to join you on the battlefield, and what happened was not his fault. It was not my fault either. No one is to blame. Elloriin knew the risks of taking up the sword and going into battle; she accepted those risks, but unfortunately, she was a casualty of the battle. You should have stopped her."

"And how do you think I could have done that? You know as well as I do that she was very stubborn. Once she had decided to do something, she would not be gainsaid. Do you not think I tried to dissuade her? She would not listen, and so I had to accept that she would take her place on the field of combat." Malor drained his goblet, and set it down with a thud.

The wizard went to the table, picked up the bottle, and went to refill Malor's goblet.

"And now you have finally decided to rejoin us," Goldwen said.

"It is the King's command," Malor replied. He took another drink.

"You have disobeyed him before - " Goldwen began.

Malor rose to his feet angrily. "I do not wish to speak of this any more! I will leave you now." He put his goblet down and made to walk out of the garden.

"Peace!" Goldwen said, holding up his free hand.

Malor stopped, and regarded the wizard. His eyes burned with anger.

"Sit down," the wizard said. "Please, Malor."

Malor gazed at him for a moment, and then he turned and resumed his seat.

"Carry on with what you were telling me," he said curtly.

Goldwen took a draught from his goblet. He sighed as the warmth of the wine coursed down his throat. He looked into the distance, remembering. His voice took on a thoughtful tone.

"After the battle on the Great Plain, I decided to give only my personal assistance to the Men of Rewes and the Plainsmen who were hard-pressed by Malkaar's forces. There were still many of our people that wished to join me, but I did not want another Elf's death to be on my conscience, only my own if that were to be my fate, so I ordered them to stay and fortify the city and to search the forest and The Vale for Malkaar's evil-doers. This they agreed to do. I left the Council to be chaired by Serenon, another thing that Amberon hates me for, and departed."

As he stood there telling his story, he slipped into reverie as he recalled the events of those days long ago. Malor saw his eyes unfocus, and the wizard's voice seemed to come from far away, as though he had indeed returned to the past.

"When I had reached the hill above Kharamanda, I looked down and could see that the city was under siege by the Cobrans, who had become the elite soldiers of Malkaar. Going down the hill, I met a captain of foot who led me to the encampment of Men who were trying to break the siege from the rear of the Cobran lines. I offered my services in the fight, and went in the van of the foot. We attacked."

A twinge of pain ran along Goldwen's back as he recalled the desperate fight: the screams of the dying, the heavy blows and whistling flights of arrows, and the magical forces which he had used against the enemy.

"I used my powers and struck the enemy, and the Men crashed through the weakened Cobran line. Of that bitter time, I will only say that those Men fought valiantly and ferociously against a foe that asked for no mercy, and received none. The Cobrans had committed many barbarous acts of atrocity, and there was not one Man there that would forgive them. They were finally pushed back across the Great Plain. We entered the city, which was once a fair and fine dwelling-place of Men, but was now despoiled and burned by the depredations of the Cobrans. The people of the city cheered and waved in jubilation as we entered, giving us a heroes' welcome. Their spirit had not been broken. The city had held out, and became the meeting place of all the races, who were planning the counter-stroke against the enemy."

A young Elf boy entered, and bowed to Goldwen.

"Your pardon, master. Master Telewen is at the door and wishes to speak with you."

"Ah," Goldwen said. "Good. Please bring him in, Kalor. And could you ask Merilynn to bring another bottle of wine, and a goblet for our visitor?"

Kalor smiled. "At once, master." He bowed and left.

Telewen came in and greeted them both. "Goldwen," he said, "Amberon is demanding that you report to him. He wishes to take the Child of Darkness into his care." Dislike for the new head of the Council was evident in his tone.

"Did he say why?" asked Goldwen. He ran a finger around the rim of his goblet absently.

"He fears," Telewen said derisively, "that you may not be strong enough to supervise both of the children."

"Now, Telewen," said Goldwen, "I am no longer Eldest, or even a member of the Council. Amberon is your leader now, and we must accede to his will." There was a wry smile on Goldwen's face. "Please take the boy to the Eldest and give him my regards."

All three of them knew that as Goldwen's status had changed to that of just a free wizard, Amberon had no right to order his comings and goings.

"He will be incensed," said Malor.

Goldwen walked over to the bench and sat down, placing his goblet on the table. He looked up with a smile.

"Let him be. I am busy." He sat back with a sigh, revelling in the simple pleasure of being his own master and answerable to no one. He felt quite comfortable. Telewen smiled to see his disregard. When he had been Eldest, he had insisted on strict protocol in all things. Now he could relax.

Telewen's smile fell . His demeanour became serious. "You should not have stepped down, Goldwen. Several of us feel that Amberon is not fit for the task of Eldest, and this matter of Malkaar returned and the threat of the Black Circle rising again is too great for a wizard of his stature."

Goldwen rose and came to Telewen. He placed his hands on the wizard's shoulders.

"My good friend, I know that you and the others who have supported me feel that this was not the time for me to step down. But the fact remains: the power that I have given has weakened me to such an extent that I could not with any good conscience attempt to lead you."

Telewen nodded. "I understand. But there is much more to being the Eldest than just power. The knowledge that is yours has no match amongst us. And Amberon has his own desires, I am sure of it. There is something wrong about all of this. I can feel it. When the Council met, I could sense a presence in the hall. It was something evil, but only I seemed to feel that there was anything wrong. And Amberon and his friends acted very strangely. He had the air of someone who was under the spell of another."

Goldwen listened intently to his friend's worries. "Are you certain that you did not just feel their emotions?" His arms dropped to his side.

"No." Telewen shook his head. "It was something from outside the room. It floated from one to another." He paused and considered his next statement. "I even sensed it about you, especially when you told us of your decision and acted out the Ritual of Divestment." He looked at Goldwen in embarrassment.

"Do not be ashamed, Telewen. It is right that you tell me of this." He stroked his chin in thought. "Was there anything else that you noticed?"

"Yes, when -" Telewen stopped abruptly, glanced quickly at Malor, and then returned his gaze to Goldwen.

Goldwen saw the hesitation on his face, and realised that Telewen was uncomfortable because what he had to say involved Elinor's death.

"Go on, Telewen," came Malor's voice, startling the both of them. They turned to look at the Lord of Oakdean.

"Your pardon," said Telewen. Malor nodded for him to continue.

"When – when Elinor died," said Telewen, "I was watching Amberon, and he looked as if he was listening to something that only he could hear, and he and Candreen exchanged a suspicious glance. When Amberon became aware of me, he turned and glared at me. It was as though I had been caught stealing something. I stepped down to the floor to escape his scrutiny, and I have waited till now to tell you, because he and Candreen have been watching me."

Merilynn the servant girl entered carrying a tray upon which were a bottle of wine, and the goblet. Goldwen and Telewen ceased their conversation.

Merilynn placed the tray on the table.

"The wine and the goblet you asked for, master." She bowed.

"Thank you, my dear. You may go."

She smiled, bowed, and left the courtyard. The three watched her go, remaining silent until the door had been closed behind her.

Goldwen went and poured Telewen a drink. He gave the goblet of honey-wine to the wizard. Telewen took only a sip, and put the goblet down on the table. His face became troubled.

"I tell you," Telewen continued, "the way that they acted was not normal. I am convinced that there is something here that bears close investigation."

Goldwen looked out into the garden. He paced the courtyard with his hands clasped behind his back. "Strange," he said, almost to himself. He stood for a moment, lost in thought. Then he walked back to the others. "We must be on guard, my friends. If the Dark One has returned, and you sense something, Telewen, yours is the most sensitive of perceptions, and we should take heed of it. Malkaar could be trying to infiltrate the Council for some dark reason. Do not forget who it was who first spoke for him."

"Do you think Amberon is a traitor?" Malor said.

"I do not know," said Goldwen, "But we must be watchful."

"You should not have allowed him to become Eldest," said Telewen.

Goldwen stepped forward and he grasped Telewen's hands in his own. "Be assured. I shall remain here in Algol, and if the Council wishes to have my advice, I will give it."

"I believe that you will be asked for it, Goldwen. I will enjoy the look on Amberon's face when he realises that he is not rid of you just yet." Telewen smiled, nodded to them both and left to take the child to Amberon.

"Now," said Goldwen, "where was I?" He stroked his chin.

"Kharamanda?" offered Malor.

Goldwen refilled his goblet. This time, he didn't ask Malor if he wanted any wine, he just filled the other goblet and put it before his brother. Malor ignored it as Goldwen went on. He seemed to slip back into reverie.

"Ah, Yes. After the Cobrans had been driven out, we had a hurried council of war. Various emissaries and warriors represented all the Races of Erathyn, and we decided that we must push Malkaar's army right back to his stronghold and defeat him. Shaarla the wizardess put forward her plan to cast the Ice of Foreverness. Many there were dismayed to hear of such a drastic measure, and said that it must only be used as a last resort if the Army of Light failed in its attempt to crush the Dark One." He took a drink to moisten his throat, and then continued.

"We set the order and strength of our forces and marched. Anarys and Nerolynn led the army for the long journey to the Dark One's stronghold. It was made up of people from all the races, as was your own force that fought on the Great Plain. When we reached the Kharden range, our army split into two groups. The King led the force that would traverse the High Pass through the mountains, and Queen Nerolynn commanded the group that would attack the Dark One through the valley that lay at the foot of his tower. I joined Anarys and the force that went via the High Pass, and Paranon went with the Queen. But Malkaar had been waiting for us, and threw all of his strength against us. I did not have enough power to resist him as he smashed the mountainside and hurled it down upon us. Many of our host died under the deluge of rock, and I was knocked senseless and buried myself. Anarys was struck down also, and was almost slain."

The pain in his back was like knives. He recalled the avalanche of rock that had engulfed the army, and how he had been struck down, his magic not strong enough to hold back the fatal rock fall that Malkaar had unleashed. Malor looked intently at his face, seeing sweat break out as Goldwen relived those terrible moments.

"He must have felt my presence and wished to finish me . . . however, at that moment, he realised that there were not as many in our force as had been reported to him by his spies. He knew that we had only been a diversion and raced back to his tower to repel the main force. He and Paranon fought each other as the two armies joined in battle. He killed Paranon, but realised that his army was on the verge of defeat. Sacrificing his Army of Darkness to save himself, he cast a mighty Spell of Stasis over all who were in the valley. Shaarla, knowing that her time had come, cast her own spell, and gave her own life to rid Erathyn of his dark ambitions."

"And that is when the remnants of your force came back with the wounded, and you were with them," finished Malor.

Goldwen returned to the present. "Yes. Unfortunately, Malkaar had sent a great part of his forces against Algol, and in the conflict, most of the Council perished, including Serenon. Only Amberon and two lesser acolytes survived. But at least the surviving members of the Black Circle who had joined the attack were destroyed."

"This was the force that we utterly destroyed on the Great Plain," said Malor.

"Yes. The Council had not moved from Algol and did not commit the Elves to battle. This was something that the other races did not forgive, forgetting the deaths of all our warriors, and ignoring the fact that it was an Elven wizardess that had defeated Malkaar himself when all else had failed."

The only sound was the birdsong as each of them became lost in their own thoughts.

"So for the last thousand years," said Goldwen finally, "the Races of Erathyn have been drifting away from the closeness they previously enjoyed, and now we only tolerate each other and mostly stay out of each other's way. The reason for this is the War, and also Malkaar's guile, for he sowed the seeds of dissention among the races as a farmer scatters seed."

"And now," said Malor, "We must face him again." He stood and picked up the goblet, and saluted Goldwen with it. Then he drained it in one long draught, and placed it on the table with a thump. "I promise you, Goldwen, that I will pledge the people of Oakdean to defeat him. I will not rest until he is utterly destroyed. My wife, and now my only daughter have been taken from me by his evil, and I will be avenged upon him."

Goldwen put down his own goblet and faced his brother. He could see the stern resolve in every line of Malor's face. He extended his hand. This time Malor stepped forward and they clasped each other's forearms in the manner of Men.

"For them," said the wizard.

Malor nodded, and his grip tightened on Goldwen's arm.

"For them," he said grimly.

The door opened, and Kalor appeared. He came and bowed before Goldwen.

"Master. Master Telewen and Master Vandaron are here and wish to speak with you."

"Please bring them in, Kalor."

"Yes, master." He bowed and turned to go. He paused, and turned back to Goldwen.

"Should I ask Merilynn to bring another goblet, master? For Master Vandaron." The boy grinned.

Goldwen smiled. "Yes, good idea. Please do."

The boy bowed, and went out, closing the door.

The door opened, and Telewen and Vandaron appeared. The Master of Birds looked the worse for wear; his cloak and robe were rent and dirty. There were small cuts on his face, and he looked exhausted. The two wizards came into the garden and stood before Goldwen.

"Goldwen," Vandaron said, "I had expected to find you in the Eldest's tower, but Telewen tells me that Amberon has taken your place, and you have stepped down. Why have you done this?"

"I have my reasons, my friend. But they can wait." Goldwen said. "What has happened to you? What did you see?" He indicated the bench, and Vandaron gratefully sat down.

Merilynn entered, holding a goblet upon a white cloth. She came to Goldwen and bowed.

"For Master Vandaron," she said. She handed it to the wizard.

"Thank you, Merilynn. Please leave us."

"Yes, master." The girl bowed and left the garden, closing the door behind her.

Goldwen poured Vandaron a goblet of wine, and handed it to him. Vandaron drank it down in a single draught, and then he placed it on the table.

"I flew far into the North, until I reached the Dark One's old stronghold. There I landed, changed form, and looked down into the valley. The two armies that had been frozen in the last battle were as they have been for centuries. The tower still stood, but there was no ice surrounding it. As I looked closer, I could see a vast army that was camped at the foot of the tower. It was a huge host, numbering in the many thousands. They were preparing for war. I could see the Cobrans among them, and many other evil Men who were just arriving, marching in a great column. I could hear the rumour of their feet as they approached the tower. There were catapults being built, and other engines of war. The sound of hammers striking steel reached me, and every now and then a cloud of steam that told of the smith's work would rise into the sky. I knew I had to come and report what I had seen, and began the spell to return as an eagle.

"But at that moment, I felt a coldness invade the hill upon which I stood. I sensed the presence of something evil. I raised my staff to defend against what might come, and looked about me."

"'Have you seen enough?'" Enquired a cold voice.

"I turned. The Dark One was before me. He regarded me with eyes of flame; eyes that changed colour as flames in a fire do. His malevolent gaze pierced me through, and I could sense the hatred emanating from him as a palpable force. He wore the black robe of the Black Circle, and a staff was in his hand. Black flames ran down it, but it was not consumed, nor did they harm he who held the staff. He wore a bracelet on his left wrist that was fashioned like a serpent with eyes of ebon black. He appeared to be an ancient Man, but his eyes shone with a power that belied his appearance. An aura of powerful energy surrounded him.

"We regarded each other for what seemed an eternity. Each of us was waiting for the other to strike. Then he slowly began to move to the left. I went to the right, and we circled each other like hunting beasts, neither of us looking at anything but our opponent's eyes.

"Suddenly, my foot struck something, and I stumbled. Seeing an opening, the Dark One thrust his staff out, and a tongue of black flame shot towards me. Off-balance, I hurriedly raised a shield, but his attack threw me to the ground. As I tried to regain my feet, he conjured up a fireball, and hurled it at me. I deflected it with a desperate sweep of my staff, and leapt to my feet. I summoned the lightning, and sent a bolt hurtling at him. He absorbed the bolt with his staff, and laughed at me mockingly.

"The Dark One pointed his staff at me, and a ray of energy tore at my shield. It hurled me against a rock wall. The force pinned me to the rock, and suddenly another burst of energy broke through my shield. The ray was cut off, and I fell heavily, only to be raised by a gesture from my opponent. I floated into the air, and was suspended before him. He raised his left hand, and the eyes of the serpent took fire. The Dark One made a summoning gesture, and my staff leapt from my hand, and flew into his own grasp. He fixed me with a freezing gaze as my staff burst into flame in his naked hand. Malkaar held onto it as the black flames consumed it. As the fire ate it, the staff gave up a keening sound. The Dark One dropped the charred remains into the dirt, and ground them to dust beneath his boot. He lowered his staff, and I fell to the ground. As I attempted to rise, he gestured with his left hand, and suddenly it was if a mountain had fallen on me. I fell to my knees, crushed down by the energy that poured from him.

"Is this the best that the Council of Light can do?'" He sneered at me, regarding me as nothing but an errant child who had dared to stand in his way. "You've had too many years of peace, sitting eating and drinking in your hall. You've not needed to fight, so you've turned soft." His blazing eyes burned into me with a contemptuous gaze.

"You will find that the Council is still strong, Malkaar, stronger than you think. Goldwen will destroy you."

"'Goldwen?'" he echoed. "'Is he still alive?'" He laughed again, a short derisive bark. "'Good. I'll relish meeting him again.'" The Dark One smiled coldly. "'Fly back to them, little bird, and tell them what you've seen. Tell them – tell *Goldwen* - that this time, *I'll* be the one to triumph. I'll be the one who rules Erathyn. They'll be my slaves, or they'll be *dead*. Go!'"

"I watched him carefully, expecting him to attack, but he lowered his staff scornfully. The black flames that had wrapped it disappeared with a soft huffing sound. He planted its tip on the ground, and stood waiting.

"'I've nothing to fear from you,'" he said disdainfully. "'Go.'"

"Still keeping my gaze fixed upon him, I began the Spell of Change. I turned into an eagle. With a sweep of my wings, I hurled myself into the sky. Malkaar's mocking laughter followed me as I hurtled back towards Algol." Vandaron took up the goblet, and drained it.

"He defeated you?" Telewen said incredulously.

The Master of Birds put his goblet on the table, and smiled sadly.

"He was very powerful, far too strong for me. He could have slain me, but he sent me back to give the Council his warning." Vandaron met Goldwen's eye. "The power that he used, there was something of the Void about it. It was not of this world."

"Are you certain of this?" asked Goldwen.

The Master of Birds nodded. "Yes. Somehow, he has summoned some dark energy from the stars, and has bent it to his will."

Goldwen stroked his chin thoughtfully. "There are many strange and dangerous energies in the Void. We must discover what this means. Telewen."

"Yes, Goldwen?"

"Please go and fetch Vairon. We will inform him of what Vandaron has seen."

"Yes, Goldwen." Telewen walked out of the garden to find Vairon.

"Now will you tell me why you stepped down?" Vandaron asked.

Goldwen clapped him on the shoulder. "Of course, my friend." He took up the bottle.

"More wine?"

"Please." Vandaron picked up the goblet and Goldwen filled it for him.

That afternoon, the Council gathered with the other Elves who lived at Algol at the Place of Burning, which was on a hill on the side of the city that faced the river. Goldwen was there, as were Shelarindel, Lindsa, Nildoron and Malor. They had come to pay their respects to Elinor, for the Elves of Algol burned any of their own that had died from misfortune, and scattered their ashes into the Silvering.

Malor stood with the group, looking down at where his daughter lay. His face was set and hard. His eyes betrayed the fact that he was deep in thought; he remembered all the days that Elinor had been by his side. He still could not believe that she was gone. But there she was, still and cold, never to be seen or spoken to again. All he could think of was the argument that had led to this. He blamed himself, for if it had not occurred, she would still be with him; such were his melancholy thoughts. Goldwen touched his arm. He nodded abstractedly at his brother's concern, and gave him a weak smile that did not reach his eyes.

The sun was just going down before the pavilion that the Council stood in. This was a large semi-circular edifice, made with the Shaping magic of the Elves, and was about twenty feet high and opens to the sky. The walls of the pavilion were made of living oak, and were liberally covered with precious stones, which sparkled and glittered in the dying light of the sun like millions of tiny stars. The open end of it faced the bier of dead oak staves upon which the body of Elinor lay.

She was dressed in a forest green robe that flowed down the side of the bier to the ground. Her feet were bare, according to Elven tradition, and her hands were crossed in front of her chest. A strip of black cloth covered her eyes, signifying that those eyes would see no more in this world. Her unbound hair hung down in a still glorious fall of golden splendour. Malor was thankful that her face could not be seen, he wished to remember her how she been. Her death in the Tower of Cherrdelion burned with raw pain in his heart.

The Council stood at intervals along the edge of a dark green marble pavement.

Amberon, (or the Eldest now) stood in their midst with the belt of office around his waist and a satisfied look on his face. Now that he was Eldest, the look said, he would change quite a few things. Next to him was Candreen, his face showing content in his master's good fortune. Beside him was the Child of Darkness, dressed in the grey of a lesser acolyte. The Child of Light stood next to Goldwen silently. Neither of the two children had yet spoken, although they now looked about fifteen years old, but both of them listened intently to the muted conversations around them.

An honour guard stood forming an aisle that led to the bier. They wore full armour, which glistened in the failing light and they held spears at rest. In two ranks outside of them were Elven trumpeters, standing with their long silver horns by their sides. Pennants hung from the horns, marked with the different Orders of the guard.

As the sun set in the mountains, a guard of the Order of the Rose came forward bearing a torch. He paced down the aisle of guards and approached the bier. He stood before the pyre with the torch held out in front of him. He turned and looked at the Eldest, waiting for a signal.

The Eldest raised his hand. As he did this, the trumpeters raised their horns and a fanfare rang out fair and bright in the still air. To Malor's ears, however, the horns sounded harsh, braying in the stillness.

Amberon proclaimed loudly; "We return this our sister to the Primal Elements. Her eyes do not see, her ears do not hear. Her heart does not beat. Her feet do not press the ground, for she does not walk. Her hands do not touch, nor make. Her voice is not heard. She has departed." His voice rolled out into the dusk, echoing against the walls of the pavilion. Malor shuddered as he heard it, his hands clenched into fists. Goldwen looked sideways at him, but held his peace.

The Eldest then let his hand fall. The guard raised the torch in salute, and then placed the burning end into the pyre, which caught instantly. He backed away. The honour guard crashed to attention, their spears coming to their shoulders in salute. The flames began to creep up the bier and ignited the robe in which the body was swathed. They began to advance. Malor closed his eyes as they covered the bier and its burden. Soon the girl's body was hidden in roaring flame. The Elves stood in respectful silence, the lurid glare of Elinor's funeral pyre flickering on their faces and making the shadows dance eerily. The Lord of Oakdean opened his eyes, wishing for one last sight of his beloved daughter. He felt the tears well up, and then they spilled down his cheeks. Everything blurred in his sight as he wept openly. Others there followed suit. Shelarindel came to his side, and reached out her hand to him. He took it, and they stood together giving each other comfort.

Goldwen felt eyes upon him. He turned and saw the Child of Darkness gazing intently at him, like some bird of prey as it stoops upon its victim. The flame was reflected in his eyes as though they were made of some dark metal. He heard a voice whisper "*Mother*". The Child of Light stood beside him, and tears flowed down his face. Goldwen put his arm around him. He turned at once from the flames and hid his face in the wizard's robe. The Child of Darkness turned away. His look held disdain for his brother's weakness, and as his gaze travelled down to the funeral pyre, he smiled to himself. Only Goldwen noticed.

CHAPTER IV

THE BALANCE OF MAGIC

After the body of Elinor had been disposed of in the ceremony, the ashes were gathered and taken down to the river's edge and cast onto the sparkling water. The entire gathering stood and watched silently, giving their respect. Goldwen looked down at the Child of Light who was clutching his arm. The wizard waited for him to speak again, but he did not say another word.

Candreen came over to them. He bowed before them and delivered a message.

"Goldwen, the Eldest has instructed me to summon you to a meeting of the Council." He looked at the others. "Lord Malor, you and the Lady Shelarindel are also asked to come."

Goldwen was mystified. Why would his brother and Shelarindel be asked to attend? "Tell the Eldest we will come," he said.

Candreen bowed and left them. They turned away from the river and walked back past the pavilion, a quiet group; all of them were lost in their own thoughts and memories of the unfortunate Elinor. Night had fallen. The group left the Place of Burning as the moon rose slowly above the range of mountains. The honour guard and the trumpeters marched away. The Child of Darkness went with the Eldest and his servants.

Lindsa and Nildoron returned to the tower that had been allotted to Goldwen, taking the Child of Light with them. He made no sound, being deep in grief, but as he turned to leave, he looked into Goldwen's eyes. The wizard could feel his suffering.

Goldwen watched them lead the boy away, and then he and Malor and Shelarindel turned and headed towards the Eldest's tower that was in the middle of the city. All of the towers of the Council of Light formed the points of an eight pointed star, which radiated out from the park in Algol's centre. They all stood in a line forming the outer edge of a circle, and the Tower of Cherrdelion was at the Eastern apex of that circle. Then, beginning in a clockwise direction, spaced in even intervals, the towers were occupied by firstly; the Master of Earth Magic, then the Master of Air Magic, the Master of Fire Magic, the Master of Water Magic, the Master of Void Magic, the Master of Birds, and finally, the Master of Beasts. As Amberon was the Eldest, his tower was now designated as the Eldest's.

Goldwen and his companions walked down the path and joined the Eldest and the Councillors who were waiting for them in front of the Eldest's tower. They entered and made their way to the main audience chamber reserved for such meetings. The large oaken door that marked the entry to the chamber displayed the sigil of the Council on it. The Eldest's boy servant Ari opened it, and bowed respectfully as they all entered. The chamber was a large circular room, with rich tapestries that hung from the walls that were embroidered with the language of magic in High-Elven script. A long, oval table made of oak stood at the far side of the room with seven chairs set along the opposite side facing the door. The largest of these, the Eldest's, was at the centre, with the other chairs on either side. Above this chair hanging upon the wall was a large banner that displayed the seal of the Council in silver and gold.

The Eldest took his chair and the Council the others, leaving Goldwen and his companions standing before them. Candreen stood behind the Eldest and to his right hand. Several large candles in tall stands illuminated the room and filled the air with glowing amber light. Silence fell as the door was closed behind them. Malor and Shelarindel exchanged a glance and wondered why they were there.

"Lord Malor," began the Eldest, "We sorrow for your loss. Please accept the Council's sympathy."

"I thank you and the Council, Eldest." Malor placed his hand over his heart and bowed. "I have pledged the people of Oakdean to support you in this matter."

"We accept your support. His Majesty will be joining us to see the children for himself. Are we to understand that you and your brother are reconciled, and that you and your people will rejoin us in the return to Glindarion?"

Malor glanced at his brother. "Indeed, Eldest. Once that we are certain that the Dark One is destroyed, we will leave this world along with all of our folk."

The Eldest smiled. "That is good to hear. His Majesty will be pleased that you have accepted his will. Our time on this world draws to a close. We will leave it to Men."

"They will be welcome to it, Eldest." Malor bowed again to the Council. Goldwen at his side gave him a smile. He was sure that Goldwen was as pleased as Amberon was. Malor also knew that the Eldest shared his view of Men and was happy with his decision.

The subtle power that had invaded the Tower of Cherrdelion slowly formed in the air. It hovered like an unseen mist above the table. Telewen looked slowly around the room as he sensed its strangeness. He attempted to locate it as the Eldest addressed the healer.

"Lady Shelarindel. Is this Child of Light really good and not evil? The Council would be certain that there is no danger from two creatures of the Dark One." The Eldest waited for her to answer. The energy drifted down to him.

Shelarindel looked at the faces of the Councillors. She had never thought that she would stand here before them. They knew that she did not hold them in esteem, for it was to join them that Goldwen had forsaken her. Now she would show them that Goldwen, in her eyes, was better than they were.

"Eldest, Masters, I have complete trust in Goldwen that when he said that he imbued the Child of Light with his own power for the good of Erathyn, he spoke truly."

The unseen presence surrounded the Eldest. The cold Voice spoke again in his mind: *Then this child is no threat...*

"Then you do agree with him that this child is no threat?"

Shelarindel looked the Eldest straight in the eye. "I agree with all my heart." The Council could feel her scorn, and also the love that she still bore the wizard.

Telewen tried to attract Goldwen's attention, but the former Eldest's eyes were fixed on Shelarindel.

"It is of no matter..." Amberon heard.

"Very well. We thank you, My Lady." Amberon saw the look of gratitude pass between Goldwen and the healer.

Shelarindel bowed to them. The Eldest's gaze swept the table.

"Then do we all agree that Goldwen shall be the teacher of this boy?"

The Council all concurred that this should be so. The Eldest nodded.

"So be it," he said. "Goldwen, the Council appoints you the guardian and teacher of this child."

Telewen's raised eyebrows and imploring look caught Goldwen's eye. The Councillor wordlessly expressed by his glance that he could feel the presence again. Goldwen tried to sense it himself. He could detect nothing unusual. Could Telewen be right? He returned his attention to the Council.

Goldwen bowed. "I thank you, Eldest, Masters."

"We would also ask something else of you, Goldwen. Even though you have stepped down, you still have great knowledge of magic. The Council would like you to have the position of advisor, to assist us and give your opinions. It would still be a position of importance, if not as lofty as your previous one." He spoke condescendingly, taking pleasure in the fact that now it was he, not Goldwen, who was the Eldest. None in the chamber missed his patronizing tones. He smiled at Goldwen unctuously.

Goldwen chose to ignore the sarcasm in his voice. "I would be pleased to continue to serve," he said. He saw the smiles from Telewen and Vandaron. Vairon and Vandaron also nodded to him, indicating their support, confirming the conversation that they, Goldwen and Telewen had had in the garden earlier.

The Eldest's satisfaction was slightly diminished when he saw that Goldwen would not react to his gibe. His smile fell. It did not matter. It was still he and not Goldwen who now sat in the seat of power.

"The power is now yours...He is nothing..." Indeed. Goldwen could have no influence on him or the Council now. The promise had been fulfilled.

Telewen glanced at the Eldest again. He was sure there was something there. Goldwen appeared not to sense it, but he was certain of it. He turned to Goldwen, his questioning look waiting for an answer. Goldwen slightly shook his head in negation. Telewen turned and stared at Amberon, as if the force of his gaze would reveal to him the invisible power.

"The first thing I would advise us to do is to prepare to attack the Dark One and his army," said Goldwen. "If he is indeed as powerful as Vandaron has told us, and his army as vast as he described it, we must move against him soon."

Amberon gave Goldwen a self-important look. "That is not your concern. The Council will decide how to proceed against him."

"But surely he presents a threat that must be dealt with?" Goldwen pressed.

"Be careful..." said the Voice in Amberon's mind.

"Of course he does. But surely the Council together can defeat him?" The Eldest said smoothly.

"Vandaron said that the Dark One was somehow drawing on some strange power from the Void. It is not the same as the sorcery that he used that we have faced before. I think that this makes the matter more pressing. We cannot afford to allow Malkaar to build up his forces for an attack that we may not be able to resist. Vandaron said that the Dark One's power was immense. Is that not true, Vandaron?"

The Master of Birds looked uncomfortable. "Yes. My strongest magic was of no avail against him. He defeated me as though I were only a mere acolyte. I think Goldwen is right, we must make preparations to face him."

"All in good time, my friends," Amberon said. "First we will deal with these children. The Dark One and his army can wait."

"But Malkaar is amassing his forces now," said Goldwen. "We cannot allow him to do so —"

The Eldest held up his hand, cutting him off. "Remember your place, Goldwen," he said coldly. "You are no longer in charge, or even a member of the Council. We appreciate your advice, but I have decided that the Dark One and his army are a lesser evil than this child that he has created. We will deal with that first. We have time enough to deal with Malkaar later." He leaned forwards. "When it was you who sat here in the postion of Eldest, I did not disobey any of your commands. I would expect to receive the same deference from you."

Goldwen bowed. "Of course, Eldest. I meant no offence."

Amberon smiled. "Thank you." He sat back, pleased that he had shown Goldwen up in front of the Council. He had put Goldwen in his place, and in front of Shelarindel, too. He knew that the healer blamed the Council for the love that she bore Goldwen that Goldwen had not seen fit to return. He glanced at her. She was quite beautiful, but the love of a mere woman was as nothing next to being Eldest. Again he congratulated himself on his newly won position.

"Brothers," he continued, "let us now turn to the matter of the other child." Amberon placed his elbows upon the table in front of him and steepled his fingers beneath his chin. "As we know, thanks to Goldwen, the signs that we have seen clearly show that somehow Malkaar has escaped from his prison and the sorcery that he has used against our people must be answered." The Council members nodded and made signs of agreement.

"You will train the boy..."

"Also, I think that we have a great opportunity to create an ally in our cause, and it is for this reason that I will train and supervise the Child of Darkness myself." The Council murmured at this, shifting in their seats.

"But Eldest," Telewen protested, "Is that wise? We know that the one who created him is powerful. We do not yet know why he has done this. Surely the boy is dangerous?"

The Eldest turned to him, saying: "Do not worry, Telewen. He is only a boy, and I will handle him. As for the Dark One, surely together we can match him?" The Eldest spread his hands, indicating the whole Council.

Goldwen heard the words in disbelief. Amberon had been against encountering the Dark One before this. Now he thought that the Council could face and destroy him. It was a change of outlook that was not normal. Goldwen knew that of all of them, Amberon was the one who was least in control of his emotions, but Amberon was not one to allow his weaknesses to show. What could have changed his mind and his attitude towards Malkaar? Goldwen caught Telewen's eye. Maybe this was a part of what his friend could sense? Telewen nodded once emphatically. There seemed to be something strange about Amberon.

Goldwen addressed him. "Why should you alone take the Child of Darkness under your supervision?"

The Eldest smiled. "Now, Goldwen, You know as well as I that these two children are very different from any of our other students. I will take the boy to see that he receives the proper guidance that he requires."

"Students? Should not the Council keep the child under a Spell of Binding until we should learn the mind of our enemy?" Goldwen folded his arms and all in the room sensed power radiating from him. The momentary perception faded.

"You are the strongest..."

The Eldest spread his hands magnanimously. "I am still but a servant of the Council and of Algol, Goldwen. However, I am the strongest now. It would seem logical for me to be the one." He paused, then said; "I think that we can use this to our own advantage. The boy can be trained in magic, and he could be turned to our side against Malkaar." He leaned back in his chair. "Besides, your *creation* should see to it that the Balance is not disrupted. I am quite certain that due to the great exertions that you have made, you could not handle the two children by yourself. So I will let you supervise the Child of Light, as long as the Council and I are satisfied with the way that you proceed."

"I am honoured. But I do not agree that you should instruct this child in the mysteries."

"He has given up his rights..."

The Eldest sat forward in his chair. "You do not have any say in what I or the Council do any more, Goldwen. You have given up those rights. I give the other child to you because you created him." His eyes glittered. "But, I warn you, do not seek to oppose me..."

To all the others in the chamber, it seemed that a great force strained between them; as if they were fencing with swords of thought. They held each other's gaze as the Eldest strove to impose his will upon Goldwen's. To Malor's amazement, it seemed that Goldwen could still resist, even though he had appeared weak. The Council itself was surprised at this remnant of power; when Goldwen had stepped down, they thought that he was finished as a wizard. Shelarindel and Malor also wondered at the hidden reserve of strength. To them, Goldwen had also seemed stripped of his former power.

As the duel of wills continued, Goldwen felt a tingling begin in his lower back. The last time that he had felt such a pain had been when he had faced the Dark One all those years ago. His intense gaze pierced the Eldest as he attempted to keep control over the sharp twinges that steadily became worse. Sweat stood out on his brow, but he noted with some satisfaction that Amberon's face was shining with sweat also.

A feeler of the dark power reached out to him to add its assault to the Eldest's. However, it recoiled when it felt the strength that still lay deep within the wizard. It withdrew to Amberon's side, and he gasped as he felt it leave him. He realised that alone he was still no match for his former master.

The atmosphere grew tense. Clearly, the two had fought before and often; as will any two whose personalities are not in accord, and who are both reluctant to give in. For a moment longer, the two held each other's stare, and then suddenly Amberon lowered his eyes. Goldwen drew in a deep breath, and exhaled it in a sigh. The tension in the chamber drained away. Could there be something of the Dark One in this attack? Was Telewen correct? He looked over at his friend, who indicated that he thought the same thing.

"He still has power...Beware...," whispered the voice in Amberon's mind.

"Enough," said the Eldest. His eyes were steely as he glared at Goldwen, and his face showed the flush of his anger. He could not understand how Goldwen could resist him. Clearly he was not as weak as he had seemed. It was inexplicable.

"Does the Council agree that you should attempt to instruct this child?" Goldwen asked. "What do they say?"

The Councillors sat and thought. No one seemed to want to be the first to speak. Malor and Shelarindel stood there uncomfortably. They were surprised and shocked to have witnessed the battle of wills. Goldwen waited in expectation. The silence lengthened. Finally, Korwen cleared his throat. He rose from his chair.

"Eldest," he said, "I agree with you that you should take this child into your keeping. You are now our leader. Goldwen has no say in this." He sat back in his chair. The Eldest nodded in approval.

"I agree also," said Narwen. "This is none of his concern." The Master of Earth magic had always been Amberon's supporter.

"I do not agree," said Vairon. The Eldest turned a frowning face to him. "The Dark One is very dangerous. Eldest, we must find out what he has in mind, where this child figures in his plans." His imposing figure lent power to his voice, which rolled out in a deep baritone.

The Eldest considered Vairon's opposition. He knew that he had always been on Goldwen's side. The Master of Birds caught his eye. "What do you say, Vandaron?"

"Vairon is right. It would be foolish to attempt to turn this child without further knowledge of Malkaar's plans. I think we should bind him, as Goldwen says."

That left only Telewen to speak. The position of Master of Void magic had not been filled since Goldwen had stepped down, so his voice was the last.

"I know what your opinion is," said the Eldest coldly. He felt anger rising in him; at the Councillors who would not support him: Telewen, Vairon, and Vandaron. Without a majority, they could not agree. Then he remembered Candreen. He smiled secretly. Goldwen noticed it, and wondered what he was up to.

"*Now is the time...,*" whipered the voice. The unseen energy swirled around the figures of Candreen and Amberon in anticipation.

"Brothers," said the Eldest, "We have voted on what to do with this child. There are three votes for, and three against. Usually, such an impasse would leave us no choice but to send to His Majesty for a solution."

He stood and beckoned to Candreen to come forward. Suddenly Goldwen realised what he was about to do. He unfolded his arms and stepped closer to the table. He pointed at Candreen.

"He cannot vote, Amberon. He is *not* a member of the Council." Goldwen cursed himself for not seeing this before. He looked into Candreen's smiling face. "He has not completed the Level. He may advise the Council, but he has no say."

The Eldest smiled at him. "Oh, but he *has* completed the Level and the Ordeal," he said. "He is the new Master of Void magic, so he does indeed have a say." With a triumphant flourish, Amberon gestured to Candreen, turning and nodding quickly. Candreen gave Goldwen the sneer of a superior as he took off the grey robe, and dropped it to the floor. Beneath it, he was wearing a Councillor's robe. It was marked with the black sigils on the lapels that signified his specialty was in Void magic. The Councillor's were taken aback. That is, except for Amberon's confederates. They already knew of Candreen's changed status.

"As such, he certainly does have a vote in these proceedings." As though he were acting in a play, Amberon addressed Candreen. "Tell us, brother, what do you say about this child?" He turned back to see the effect of Candreen's words on Goldwen.

In mock solemnity Candreen placed his hands over his heart and said; "I have listened to your votes and opinions, brothers. But I must concur with Narwen and Korwen when they say that they are of the same mind as the Eldest. He should be the one to take this child into his keeping and tutelage."

The Eldest's gaze travelled the table, noting the reactions of the Councillors. He knew which were for him, and who were against. He would remember.

"I believe that makes the vote four against three, and as such, it is a majority. What I said stands. I have decided what I will do with this child, and that is the end of the matter." Amberon's eyes were fixed on Goldwen's face. He smiled to himself in pleasure as he watched Goldwen's anger rising.

"He is beaten...You have what you have always wanted..."

Amberon's delight in defeating his former master showed clearly on his face. The invisible presence hovered between him and

Candreen, seeming to give off an almost palpable sensation of deep satisfaction.

Goldwen rose from the table, his eyes locked on Candreen. The other returned his gaze with a haughty stare. Goldwen suddenly realised that this was what Amberon had been plotting all along. With Candreen in his own former position, and the other two wizards as his confederates, he could make the Council accept any of his proposals. A part of him grudgingly admired the smoothness with which it had been done. Another part lamented that he had not foreseen the extent of Amberon's ambition. He stepped back. Amberon's triumph showed on his face.

"Beware, *Amberon*, that it is not the end of *you!*" Goldwen said. He turned and swept out. His companions followed him, hastily bowing in trepidation to the Council and hurried after him. Ari had been listening outside to all that had been said, and as he heard their approach, threw open the door. Goldwen and the others went past him in a whirl of robes, as he stood bowed with a sheepish look on his face. He turned and shut the door, which closed with a thud like an exclamation. The Council sat silently, stunned at the display. Amberon, however, rose from his chair and stood fuming, his face burning. His eyes thinned to slits, from which a gleam of malice showed. He had never dared confront Goldwen himself in such a way before, not when Goldwen was Eldest, and especially not in front of the Council. Poison stirred in his heart and impotent anger flashed through him. Then he remembered his victory with Candreen and congratulated himself on their plotting.

"*Well done...*" said the Voice of Malkaar. Then the power withdrew and floated in pursuit of Goldwen and his companions.

The Eldest had an impression of evil laughter in his mind as the force left them. He saw that Candreen had sensed it too. They shared a conspirational smile. Then Amberon saw the puzzled look on Telewen's face. He was staring at both of them, his face perplexed. Could he have sensed the voice too? Again the thought came that the Master of Fire magic may be dangerous. He exchanged a knowing look with Candreen. He would not let anyone destroy his plans now.

Goldwen stormed out of the tower, his face a study in anger, and the only sound was their quickened breathing and the firm stride of

Goldwen's tread as he descended the steps and approached the front door. His companions hurried after, their footsteps pattering across the marble. Closely behind them came the dark energy of his adversary. As Goldwen and Malor and Shelarindel left the tower, Goldwen laughed to himself. His entire mood seemed to change in a moment. He seemed in fine spirits. The others looked at him in astonishment.

"Goldwen?" said Malor, "What is wrong with you?" Malor had not seen his brother like this before, and the incident in the tower had been unsettling, to say the least.

Goldwen stopped. "My friends," he said, "That was excellent. I now understand how Amberon felt when I was Eldest and he could not go against my will." He stroked his chin and saw the concern written on their faces. "Do not worry. I know him, and I realise that he will be furious for a time, but he is still in awe of me, and I do not believe he will do anything rash." He looked back at the tower and smiled. Then his smile faded as he thought of how Amberon had raised Candreen into his place.

The imperceptible cloud of Malkaar's will enveloped the trio unsensed. It concentrated itself around Goldwen, sending its dark tendrils into his mind.

"I must give him credit for his manoeuvre with Candreen though. It was skilfully done." He paused, deep in thought. Malor and Shelarindel waited for him to speak again. Finally, he continued, as if talking more to himself than to them. "The Council must be on their guard. He can be very persuasive. And this matter of the Child of Darkness. Surely Amberon is not foolish enough to think that he is a match for him? There is something strange about this."

"It is no longer your concern..."

It was true. His time as Eldest had passed, of his own volition. He was now only an advisor to the Council, not a member. The Child of Light needed his guidance and teaching. That was more important.

"Leave Amberon to his plots...Your task lies with the Child of Light..."

Indeed. In the conflict to come, his own *creation*, as Amberon had sneered, would be the protector of all Erathyn, and it was up to him to ensure that the boy realised the full extent of his powers. *I will teach him.* He came out of his musings.

"Come, friends," he said, "All of that debate has given me a thirst."

He smiled at the others and continued on his way. Malor and Shelarindel exchanged a look of bafflement, and then they followed after him. None of them had been aware of the presence that had whispered into Goldwen's mind, which now faded away.

When they came to the tower Goldwen had been given they entered and made their way to the dining chamber. As they walked along the hall, they could hear voices in conversation ahead of them. One voice was clearly that of Nildoron, another Lindsa's. The other they could not place. It was rich and musical, and a sense of power accompanied it. They entered the chamber, and saw the speakers. Lord Nildoron sat at one end of the table. He was toying with a goblet and looked as if he was about to answer a question. He paused as they came in. Next to him was Lindsa, who sat quietly in the attitude of one who listens with great interest.

In the other chair sat an Elf that Goldwen and his companions did not know. He was tall and noble, and had an aura of power about him. His face was serene, his eyes an electric blue that held golden flecks deep within their compass. They burned with the inner fire of magic. His long hair that hung down his back was a fine golden-yellow that shone in the candlelight, and he wore a plain grey robe. All in the chamber could sense the energy that emanated from him. He rose and bowed deeply.

"Greetings," he said, and his voice was smooth and good to hear. "What is it that you want of me?" He was the Child of Light, and he looked to be about fifteen years of age.

CHAPTER V

AWAKENINGS OF POWER

The sun rose above the City of Algol in a blaze of light. Goldwen and his companions, along with the Child of Light, had spent the night in the tower that had been given to Goldwen. They sat in the dining chamber and talked together as they ate their breakfast. Birds sang outside and the air was warm, and a slight breeze sighed in the trees.

The conversation was muted and soft, in the way that one speaks in the quiet of the morning, although Goldwen realised that the presence of the child himself made all of them hesitant to speak also. The amazing fact of his and his brother's rapid birth and growth was obviously on everyone's mind. The youth himself, though, sat in an agony of frustration. Goldwen had asked him to sleep and had said that he would explain everything to him in the morning. Now that the morning had finally come, his mind burned with questions, and he turned to Goldwen.

"Who am I?" he said. There was a hush in the conversation around the table, for it was the first time since the previous night that he had spoken. The others sat in silence as the wizard considered the question and how to reply to it. Goldwen cleared his throat.

"I suppose you are my son," he said, "for it was by my magic that I created you out of what Malkaar had done to Elinor." Goldwen stroked his chin and went on. "Once I had realised that it was indeed Malkaar's sorcery that had done this terrible thing, and that I had not power enough to destroy it, I decided that I would use Malkaar's own sorcery against him. I created a champion who would protect Erathyn, and all of us, and in the end, destroy his evil once and for all time. That champion is you." His face was kindly as he spoke, and he smiled at the child.

"You see, magic of itself is neither good nor evil. I am not talking of Shaping, but of the Elemental magic that the members of the Council practise. You should think of this magic as though it was water. It can be used for washing or drinking," He paused. "Or you can boil someone alive in it." Shelarindel winced. "It has no good or evil in it, it is only power to be used. Intention is what is good or evil. It is all a part of the Balance."

"The Balance?"

Goldwen thought for a moment, and then went on: "What we call the Balance is a force of nature that has an equalizing effect upon all things. It ensures that when we experience bad times, things never descend to absolute evil, or when times are good, such as they have been, it also does not allow us to go on in a paradise. In essence, the Balance is there to make sure that Erathyn goes on in what we call the Middle Way, which is not so bad as to make us the prisoners of Darkness, neither does it let us be so good as to be beyond reproach.

"In other and simpler words, it makes us live with both good and bad in equal doses. That is why, when I discovered Malkaar's magic, I created you, the Child of Light, for I sensed that the Child of Darkness's powers were far beyond my own, and the Balance dictated that there must be someone who could face him."

"But *who* am I?" The boy's face was set in a puzzled frown. "I think I can understand how the magic was done, but why am I the one to carry out this task? We have been alive for only a few days, and yet both I and my brother can understand and speak, and I can see that this and the way that we have grown is a frightening thing to you." His face was a study in confusion. "Do I have a name?" he said, "Or am I just an instrument of justice to you?" He bowed his head and stared down at the table.

Goldwen reached across to him and took his hand. The Elf looked up, and again the wizard was struck by his penetrating stare.

"Of course you should have a name," said Goldwen. "You are a part of me, and for you and the greater good of all, I have stepped down from the Council, so that I may train you and teach you all I know." He paused for a moment, and could see that the child had warmed to his compassion. He smiled to himself. "I will give you a name, if you will allow me."

The boy nodded.

"Then from now on, you shall be known as Malin." Goldwen looked at Malor, who nodded his agreement, for Malin had been Goldwen's name before he had taken his Name of Power, and had left his old name and life behind. Shelarindel smiled also, a little wistfully, for that name evoked powerful memories in her of many years past.

"Malin," the boy said. "I like it." He brought his other hand up and clasped Goldwen's hands. The wizard smiled, and the youth, now Malin, smiled back.

Goldwen leaned forward. "Sounds strong, does it not?" He said, and began to laugh. Malin's smile broadened. The others looked at him, trying to judge his reaction. He laughed, and the tension in the room was broken, and they all joined him. The laughter began as relief, then became a real expression of their humour, and more importantly, of their acceptance of Malin as part of their group.

Goldwen stood and held out his goblet of wine. "Malin!" he cried. They all responded and toasted Malin, who sat beaming at them.

After they had finished their breakfast, Goldwen took Malin up to a room at the very top of the tower. He indicated two chairs by the window and they sat down facing each other. Goldwen leaned back and stroked his chin.

"Where to begin?" he mused. "Well..." He gathered his thoughts, then continued as if reading aloud from a text that he had learnt by heart: "All Elven magic is based on the harnessing and use of the five elements; Earth, Air, Fire, Water, and Void."

Malin nodded. He listened attentively.

"These are the order and strength of such energies. Earth is the First element. Earth stands. It is the foundation and bedrock of all things. Without it, there could be no stability."

Malin said, "Go on."

"Air is the Second element. Air moves. It is formless, but can be powerful. A storm can uproot the strongest tree. It also gives us life. Without air, all things would die. It is always moving, restless and unseen.

"Fire is the Third element. Fire burns. It consumes voraciously. Energy burns in its heart. It is also changeable, like Air, but unlike Air, it can be seen in its many shifting forms.

"The Fourth element is Water. Water flows. It is ceaselessly moving. But its power cannot be held. Even drops of it will eventually wear away the strongest stone. Water can turn a mountain into dust. Also, much of our body is water, so it too is essential for life.

"The last element is the Void. The Void centres. All matter is mainly void, or space. It only seems to be solid to us, but in reality, all that we can see and touch is made up of minute particles. At the centre of all things, there is nothing, the Void. Do you follow me so far?"

"Yes," said Malin. "So all of the Elven magic is created by the use of such elements?"

Goldwen smiled. "That is correct. And all of the elements have Levels that are attained by the adept in his pursuit of knowledge. The First Level is Earth, and then Air and so on, until the final level, the Void, is reached. The Council have mastered all of these Levels, and have elected to stand for that element which they embody."

"What of the other two Councillors; the Masters of Birds and Beasts?" inquired Malin. "They do not represent any element."

"The Master of Birds and the Master of Beasts are also adepts, having completed all of the Levels. However, they represent these creatures with their shape shifting abilities, so that the Council can maintain contact with all animal life. The birds and beasts have many things to teach us as well. They act purely on instinct and they never lie. They never kill needlessly, and they maintain the Balance. Also, numerically and magically speaking, the number seven is more powerful than the number five, so these positions are held to make the power of the Council complete as a power of seven."

The wizard noticed with satisfaction that his pupil was absorbing all that he said. He could see that Malin had an inquiring mind, and was quick to retain knowledge. He was pleased that his intervention in Malkaar's spell seemed to be turning out to the Elves advantage. He wondered how much he should tell Malin about his role. He had thought that he had reasoned out why Malkaar had done this thing, but he still could be certain. He continued with his instruction.

"We will begin to develop the power within you and I will show you how to utilise the different elements. To do any magic you must first understand these principles, for the elements dictate the forces according to their uses. It is this knowledge that will allow you to defeat Malkaar and your brother."

"I understand," said Malin, "But do you think that the powers that you gave me will be sufficient to face him? Are you even sure that my brother will go against me?"

"You have most of my previous strength and powers, which are prodigious. I do not think, once you learn to use them wisely, that you will have any trouble. Also, Malkaar has definitely created your brother with some mischief to Erathyn in mind, and as you are with us and on the side of good, and he on the side of evil, you must face each other."

"Can we be certain that he is on the side of evil?"

Goldwen could see the doubt in Malin's eyes. He could understand the reticence in the youth's desire not to set himself in conflict against his own brother.

"I am sorry," he said, "The emanations of Dark Magic are strong around him. I am sure that Malkaar has invested evil in him, in the same way that I have given you the powers and outlook of good."

Malin accepted this reluctantly. "Why then should the Eldest take charge of my brother? Does he really think that he can turn him to your cause and against Malkaar?"

"I do not know. I believe that the Eldest may *think* that he can accomplish such a thing, but I do not feel he is strong enough. It is a conceit of his." Goldwen turned to the window where the sun sent warm rays through the glass onto the floor. He was in deep thought for a moment, and then he turned back to Malin.

"Can you feel the presence of magic within you?" he asked. "It should feel like a cold fire burning deep within your body." Goldwen studied the other intently, and Malin felt as if his very being was now subject to the most minute scrutiny that he had felt, even more so than when he and his brother had been brought before the Council. This was indeed true.

"I can feel...something," he replied.

"Well, then. *Catch this!*" Goldwen hurled a small dagger that he had secreted in his robe with a flick of his wrist. It sped toward Malin's face who sat not six feet away. Malin cried out and threw his hands up instinctively. There was a vivid flash as the dagger hit something unseen with a ringing sound. It skittered away across the floor and spun to a stop. Malin felt a tingling sensation in his hands fade away.

Malin heard a chuckle and peered through his hands, still held in front of his face.

Goldwen grinned at him thoughtfully. "Not bad," he said. "A good demonstration of the element of Earth. It can be used as a shield against physical attack."

Malin turned over his hands and stared at them in wonder.

Goldwen rose to his feet, groaning as he did so. His old injury from the Last Battle still pained him. After many years, he had learned to live with it, and had never taken time to seek out a healer. He had always been busy with the Council. He gritted his teeth as the pain intensified.

Malin looked at him in concern. He stood and came over to his mentor.

"It will pass," Goldwen rasped.

Malin looked down at his hands again. He came forward. Goldwen waved him away, but Malin ignored him. He walked around the wizard and stood behind him. Then he closed his eyes, and extending his hands before him, he swept them down over Goldwen's spine. A green glow radiated from them, soothing to look at. A tingling began in the wizard's lower back, which rapidly spread up his backbone to his neck and head. Goldwen felt a great heat, as though a burning coal had rolled along his back, and he cried out in amazement. He felt as if he were grasped by the hair and pulled upward. It was as though he was being stretched to his body's limit. There came some harsh cracking sounds, and Goldwen felt the heat abate and die away. He stood straight, without any pain at all. For the first time in many years, he was free of it! He turned and faced Malin in astonishment.

Malin stood there, sweat running down his face. He looked as if he had just run a great race. He released a sigh and lowered his hands by his side.

"How did you do that?" Goldwen asked, amazed.

Malin shook his head. "I do not know," he said. "I just felt that I could help you. I felt the power, and... I do not know."

"Do you know that only Elven women are healers?"

Malin shook his head. "What does it mean?" He stood there bewildered, as if he had no idea of what he had just done.

"I am not sure," said the wizard, "However, it shows that you have compassion."

Malin smiled at him.

"Also," he continued, "It is a good demonstration of power." He stretched, marvelling that he could do so without pain. "I thank you," he said. Goldwen was amazed and gratified that his pupil could show such ability. He would have to discuss this with the Council. A smile came to his face as he thought of the look on Amberon's face as he told him of Malin's special power. It would show that his faith in the youth was justified.

"Now," he said, "The properties of Earth..."

Meanwhile, in the tower of the Eldest, the Child of Darkness and the Eldest himself had been talking away the morning and all through the day. They sat in the Eldest's audience chamber, and Neldriin kneeled beside the Eldest and awaited his demands. Their discussion, however, was not as Goldwen's and Malin's was; as a teacher to his disciple, but more in the way of conversation between equals. This was pretence on the boy's part, for he knew that the powers that he had been given were more than a match for those that the Eldest possessed. The Eldest believed that he was in control.

Malkaar's unseen presence hovered over them. Neither of them sensed it, oblivious to the fact that the Dark One watched and listened to all that they said.

Poor fool, thought the youth, *He thinks he is my better.* None of his thoughts showed on his face, which was set in a thin smile as he nodded at what the Eldest said. He concealed his thoughts, knowing that Amberon could read them. The Eldest, thinking that he was impressing him, wore a look of magnanimous self-importance.

"So, my boy," he said, "I feel that although Goldwen thinks that you represent a danger to Erathyn, you could prove him wrong by allowing yourself to be trained in the mysteries by me, and become a member of the Council yourself. Perhaps one day, you could even become the Eldest." Amberon was in his element. He loved a captive audience, and through his misjudgement of the youth, thought that he had the upper hand.

The boy looked at him with an unreadable dark gaze. He reclined lazily upon a couch with a small table that was within reach of his right hand, upon which lay a silver platter that was heaped with grapes. Next to it was a carafe and goblets, which contained the sweet honey-wine that the Elves were so fond of. His hand strayed ever and again to these as he nodded and smiled at the Eldest's platitudes. The invisible energy flowed down and around him, and sent tendrils into the Elf's mind.

"Enough," said the Voice.

"Enough. I am tired of your chatter."

"What?" Amberon gasped. He stared at the youth. He was shocked. The boy had dared to interrupt him! "I am the Eldest!" he fumed. "You will show me the respect I deserve."

The dark eyes flashed. "I am much more powerful than you are. Do not talk down to me."

Under the glare of those black orbs, Amberon faltered to a stop. He could feel the emanations of power radiating from the other like the rays of an alien sun that burned upon his flesh.

"I wish to have finer clothing than this," the youth said, gesturing at the lesser acolyte's dull grey robe. "It is not fitting for me to wear such poor stuff." He waved his hand. There was a bright flash, and a rich red tunic replaced his dull garments, and long black boots shone upon his out-stretched feet like liquid night. The Eldest stared, open-mouthed at this display of power. Taking possession of himself, he nodded approvingly.

"Very good," he said grudgingly, "You demonstrate a fine understanding of the Arts." Inwardly, however, he was dismayed at this display of power, and for the first time, he understood that he had underestimated the boy. Perhaps Goldwen had been right. They should have chained him and put a Binding Spell upon him.

"Also," said the youth, "I do not wish to be addressed as 'the Child' anymore. It is demeaning. I shall choose a name for myself." The Eldest agreed mutely.

"I wish to be known as Brack...." The Voice prompted.

"I wish to be known as Brack from now on," he said.

The Eldest smiled wryly. Brack was the name of the Man who had led Malkaar's forces in the attack on the city of Algol many years before, when the War of the Races had been at its height. The Eldest could see the aptness in the choice; this Brack was also to be the servant of Malkaar, even as the former had been.

"Very well, said the Eldest, "You shall have that name." He gave Brack a searching look, but could not probe the boy's inner thoughts. He began to feel trepidation at the prospect of Brack's powers growing beyond his and the Council's reach. His pride, however, still beguiled him into a kind of hope that he could control the youth. Brack could read all this in the emotions flickering across the Eldest's face, and was satisfied that he had put him in his place. He turned to Neldriin, his eyes flashing.

The girl felt his gaze beating upon her with an insistence that called to her deepest being. It was as though there was a great heat that lapped around her in waves of fire. She looked up and into the eyes that bore into her own with commanding presence. Her will left her as she felt a summoning call in a sensuous, calling whisper.

"Neldriin...Neldriin."

Brack sat with the look of a predatory bird as he bent his gaze upon her. The Eldest could feel the Summoning, and sat wide-eyed in his chair. It was not a common spell that was being used. He was impressed despite himself.

"Come to me," said Brack softly. The girl rose, her face locked in a glazed stare. She totally ignored the Eldest as she walked over and stood before Brack. He put out his hand and ran it down the girl's side, beginning at her hip and continuing down to her thigh, where it remained. Brack could feel the firmness of her young flesh beneath the light gown that she wore. He looked at the Eldest, his eyes glittering with a fey light. "Leave us," he said, his voice thick with lust.

The Eldest's face set in a stony glare, but he had seen the power in the other, and besides, the girl was only a servant. He stood and bowed at Brack, and took his leave, but the mocking laughter that came from Brack seemed to ring in his ears long after the door behind him shut it off.

He paced down the corridor, anger growing within him like a flame. *How dare the young upstart treat me like a fool!* He would show the youth what his position was and teach him respect. He was the Eldest!

"*Amberon . . .*"

Amberon stopped abruptly. He peered swiftly behind himself, and then scanned the corridor intently. To his relief, he was alone.

"You should not speak to me like this, it is dangerous," he said in hushed tones.

The cold Voice went on. "*There is no one else about . . .*"

Anger crept into the Eldest's voice. "They suspect something – Telewen –"

"*Fool! . . .They know nothing . . .*"

"I am certain he has told Goldwen about his suspicions. Even though Goldwen has stepped down, he is very intelligent, and his knowledge of the Arts is far greater than mine. He would be a powerful enemy."

"*I will deal with him . . . I defeated him before . . .*"

Amberon shook his head. "This time he has the Child of Light with him. He will also convince the Council and the King to move against you. They want to form an alliance with the lesser races as was done before."

"*It does not matter . . . My powers now are far beyond theirs . . .*"

"*My army is tenfold in size to that which I commanded before . . .*"

"How can that be? Your allies were scattered and destroyed."

"*I have new alliances . . . You will see . . .*"

"What of Telewen and Goldwen?"

"*I will deal with them . . . All that you need to do is mislead the Council and the others . . .*"

"They will think it strange if I do not wish to find out what you are doing. That would surely alert them to our plan."

"*But I want you to send spies. . ."*

The Eldest stood in mute stupefaction. This made no sense.

"Why? I do not understand."

"*You must confuse them . . . Cause them to argue . . . Divide them . . ."*

"I will not be able to convince them – they will –"

"*Silence!"* thundered the Voice.

Nervously he scanned the corridor again, forgetting that the Voice was only in his mind.

Malkaar hissed venomously. "*Do not forget . . . I gave you dominion over them . . . Remember our bargain."*

That bargain did not seem so attractive to him now. He began to wish that he had not agreed to it. He was merely a tool in the Dark One's hand.

"Yes," he said wearily, "I remember."

"*Good . . . I will be watching . . ."*

The sensation that Amberon had come to recognise as Malkaar's presence faded away. He sighed to himself and slowly resumed walking down the corridor, not with the angry pacing of before, but stooping slightly, as though he carried a heavy burden that was far too much for him to bear.

CHAPTER VI

WILLOWEN

The next morning after they had broken their fast, Malin and Goldwen walked down to the main gate and left the city. They crossed the bridge and went down the road towards the forest that lay perhaps three miles away. It was time for Goldwen to begin Malin's training in earnest. The day was warm and sunny, and they soon sweated freely.

Neither of the two had spoken since rising in the morning light, as though in silent agreement with each other. Goldwen leaned upon his staff, which now served him as a prop. The light in his eyes had almost returned to the powerful gaze that he was well known for. Looking deeper, however, anyone who was well acquainted with the wizard could tell that he did not possess his vigorous strengths of old. These he had given to Malin.

As for Malin, he walked without any sign of fatigue and looked about himself in good humour. After all, he was about to be tutored in the Mysteries by their greatest practitioner, and he looked forward to gaining the knowledge that only the Council was privy to. He smiled to himself, confident in his youth and in his own assessment of his powers.

Goldwen could feel the youth's confidence and smiled also. The boy would learn. Together they entered the shadowy oak-wood.

In the Eldest's tower, Brack awoke and sat up and stretched, yawning cavernously. The night had passed quite pleasantly, thanks to the company of the servant girl whose naked form lay upon the sleeping-silks next to him. He turned his gaze on her peaceful face, and a smile of contentment crossed his own countenance. He rose, reached for a ewer of water on the side table, and poured it over his head. He stood there puffing and blowing out his breath at the coldness of the water as it ran down his naked body, slicking his long, dark mane to his back and forming a pool on the stone floor. The water that sprayed from his lips made a mist in the sunlight which streamed in through the window.

Then, as though he had been bored by this simple experience, he waved his hand with a flourish, and with a flash of light he was dressed in his fine crimson garment of the previous night and his hair was oiled and perfumed and immaculately combed. His boots gleamed spotlessly upon his feet.

He looked around the room. It was the guest's bedchamber, but now that he was not distracted by Neldriin's attentions, he did not find it to his liking. A frown wrote itself across his face.

"This will not do," he murmured. Raising his arms high, he conjured forces from Outside. With a burst of magic, the room was transformed into an opulent pleasure chamber, the previously bare walls hung with richly coloured silks, worked with a delicacy hitherto unknown to Erathyn. Deep fur rugs covered the floor, and complex incenses almost too sweet burned in tall golden censers that were chased with characters of High Magic. Brack's frown disappeared, to be replaced with a smile of radiant pleasure.

Outside the Eldest's tower, the new Eldest stood, his face dark with anger as he remembered how he had been dismissed like a mere servant. He clenched his fists as he tried to master himself. His companion, himself the new Master of Void magic, watched his face with a wry smile, but it disappeared instantly when the Eldest turned to him.

"He dares to turn *me* out! I will show him his place," the Eldest fumed.

Candreen shook his head in negation.

"Eldest," he said, "You should not let this youth disturb you. Remember that we are trying to turn him into a powerful ally." His deferential manner concealed the subtle workings of his mind, which was fixed on self-interest.

The Eldest grunted. "Yes," he replied, "I know, but he is very overbearing. It would have been far better had this incident not occurred."

Candreen knew that the Eldest was not only referring to last night's events, but also that of the arrival of the brothers in the City of the Wizards. The balance of power had shifted, and although it was now in the Eldest's favour, he would have to be careful how he proceeded. So too would Candreen.

"Eldest," he said, "If these youths had not appeared, then I would not be addressing you in this manner, and you would still be under the staff of Goldwen, and he would still be the leader of the Council. As your most trusted and humble servant, I remind you that you have waited for many years to take your place as Eldest. Now you have your heart's desire. So too, I have been elevated to the place where I can ensure that whatever you suggest to the Council will be accepted."

The Eldest knew that Candreen was right and that if it could be managed; he might be able to use Brack to his own advantage. His frown disappeared as he considered his options.

The sensation of energy that they both recognized as the presence of Malkaar formed around them. They waited for the cold Voice to address them.

"*Your servant is right . . . I have given you power over the Council . . . The boy is mine . . .*"

"What do you need him for?" Asked Amberon.

"*It is not your concern . . . Remember what I have given you . . .*"

"But I cannot control him –"

"*You do not have to . . . I will call him to me . . .*"

"For what purpose?" Said Candreen.

There was silence for a few moments, which held a sense of cold anger.

"*Do not allow your servant to address me again . . .*"

Amberon and Candreen exchanged a glance filled with wariness. Amberon held up his hand as though to still Candreen's tongue. He shook his head in warning . Both of them knew how easily the Dark One was angered.

"Forgive him, Master. He is only keen to serve us."

"*I will forgive him this one time . . . Remember, Eldest, all that you have is what I have given you . . .*"

Amberon's lips turned down and his eyes flashed as he thought of his humiliating servitude to his master. "I will not forget."

"*Good . . . What has been given can also be taken . . .*"

"We will carry out our part of the bargain."

"*Excellent . . .*"

The presence faded away. The two waited until they could sense that they were alone. They returned to their conversation.

"I suppose I must let this boy have his way. Hopefully we will soon be rid of him."

"Be patient," said Candreen, "*Eldest.*" He bowed. The Eldest nodded, and his face became inscrutable. Candreen's eyes glittered as he saw Amberon was plotting his next move. He knew that they would soon both be busy, and hopefully successful.

Above them, in the guest's bedchamber, Brack stood, his eyes staring at nothing. Then, as the pair below ceased their conversation, his face reverted to its usual half-smile. *So,* he thought to himself, *the old fool still believes that he can best me. This will be enjoyable.* He turned to the bed and said in a commanding voice; "WAKE!" Instantly the girl's eyes were open, and she blinked in drowsy astonishment. Neldriin took in the situation at once, as her shocked gaze swept the room. She leapt from the bed, fixing Brack with a frigid glare. Neldriin began to weep, but then dashed the tears from her eyes with an angry swipe of her arm. Then she advanced and struck his face with a resounding slap that echoed in the room.

"*Animal!*" She hissed in icy contempt. She stood shaking in fury before him, her fists clenched. Then she dismissed him with a disdainful toss of her head. She turned on her heel and strode from the room, scorn written in every line of her naked body. Brack raised his hand to his face, which still smarted from the blow and laughed to himself. Such spirit!

Meanwhile, in the forest, Goldwen and Malin had reached a clearing. The youth thought that they were going to walk forever in the hot sun. He had preferred the shade of the forest. He looked back longingly to the cool shadows they had just left, and then turned to speak to Goldwen. The wizard had gone! A shocked look spread over his face as he hurried forward, thinking that Goldwen had carried on ahead of him.

The wizard's voice came out of nowhere, "STOP!"

Malin halted, wondering what was happening. The forest grew silent. The calls and singing of the birds were stilled, and there was not a sound. Even the wind ceased. The youth looked around the clearing, trying to find where Goldwen had gone. He saw nothing but the trees all about him. An ominous silence descended.

The voice came again: "DEFEND YOURSELF!"

Malin jumped nervously. Suddenly, from all sides of the glade, a motley group of figures appeared with drawn swords and advanced towards him menacingly. They were dirty and uncouth, their clothes were ragged, and their faces were weathered and grim. They were not Elves! Could they be Men? He was trapped!

"Goldwen!" he shouted. There was no response. Could the wizard have brought him here only to be slain by these Men? Of course not, his own father would not do such a thing!

These thoughts flashed through his mind as he watched the Men advancing towards him. Frantically he looked around for a way out. There was none. He was completely surrounded. He looked down and saw a broken branch almost at his feet. Stooping, he picked it up. It was better than no weapon at all, but against swords?

This is where I end, thought Malin. *So much for me being the champion of Erathyn.* He held the branch like a club, turning to try to keep all the Men beyond their sword's reach. He circled, his eyes fixed upon them as they closed in. They had not spoken. The only sounds were the tread of their heavy boots rustling in the fallen leaves at their feet, and the rapid breathing of their prey. Their eyes showed a blood lust normally only seen in animals. Their teeth were bared in anticipation of the kill.

Suddenly in his mind, there was a voice: *"USE YOUR MIND, BOY!"*

He lowered the branch in confusion. "Goldwen?"

The wizard's voice came again in his mind: *"WHAT WILL KEEP THEM OFF, MALIN?"*

As the Men encircled him, their swords glittered in the hot sun, ready to drink his blood. A blinding flash struck Malin in the eye as sunlight reflected from a blade. An image of Goldwen came to him, remembered from the night just passed, when he had shown Malin how to visualise and employ the different Elements. A memory of Goldwen flashed into his mind, of the wizard conjuring a flame from his open hand. Goldwen's voice came to him, saying: "*Our magic comes from three things; Thought, Word, and Deed. First you must think of the Element used and conjure its energy, the Thought. Speak its name, which is the Word, and the Deed is bringing it to life as the power flows through you.*"

A flame! Suddenly, he realised how he could protect himself. He raised the branch, conjuring in his mind the image of flame on the end of it. "*Fire!*" he cried. The branch burst into flame. He waved the branch in front of the Men, who moved back when threatened, but kept moving closer when he turned. He knew that this situation would not last, and that soon he would be brought down. Where was the wizard? Was he incapacitated, and could only speak to Malin with his mind?

As Malin thought desperately, one of the Men took advantage of his distraction and lashed out with his sword, cutting Malin's right arm. The youth flew into a rage with the pain and struck at his adversary with the branch. At the same moment, the image of fire in his thoughts grew into a conflagration that filled the universe. A vision of flame swam before his suffering gaze, and he pictured it in his anger engulfing his enemy. He was surprised when it did, with the brilliant flash that told of magic used. Out of his control, a tongue of incandescence roared from the branch, and lapped his adversary in white heat. The Man flared like a torch, screamed, dropped his weapon and fell burning to the ground. His companions halted and stood silently about Malin.

The Men hesitated as their comrade lay burning and writhing. Malin too watched the Man's agony amazed. At that moment, any of the others could have run him through, but they were also stunned, and stood with their weapons lowered. Then, horrified, Malin dropped the branch. He swayed, as the energy that the magic had required had weakened him considerably. He fell to his knees beside the body, his head bowed.

The Men recovered and began to close in again. The youth only knelt by the blackened corpse, defenceless. He seemed about to collapse and trembled in nervous shock. The first Man to reach Malin raised his sword high to cut him down. He looked up as the Man towered over him like an avenging spirit. Dimly, Malin realised he could not save himself, but he was so exhausted by his magical efforts, that it did not seem important. The sword fell, casting a shadow between his eyes, which he closed in anticipation of the fatal blow.

"HOLD!" A powerful shout came from the forest. The Men froze in position. Malin opened one eye a crack, and saw the immobile figure above him. The sword hovered over his head motionlessly as its wielder was halted in his task. If it had fallen further, his skull would have been split. The youth opened his eyes wider and peered about himself in astonishment. The other Men were a silent circle of statues.

"BEGONE!" The Men vanished, accompanied by a slight hissing sound. Only the corpse remained. From the shadows beneath the trees the wizard appeared. He came forward, until he reached Malin. The youth rose and looked down at his late adversary, now a seared, blackened skull and a pile of burnt rags from which the charred bones protruded. He looked up at Goldwen.

White with anguish, he whispered, "*I killed him!*"

The branch continued to burn, and its crackling was the only sound for a few moments. Goldwen walked over to the corpse. He looked down at it, and then met Malin's gaze with his own.

"Oh?" He said. He waved his hand over the body. It vanished, as the others had done. Malin stared. Then comprehension dawned. He grimaced distastefully at the wizard.

"Another test?"

"Another test," confirmed Goldwen. He smiled at the youth. "At first you did well. However, I am wondering why you did not just use a shield. The element of Earth is easier to invoke than that of Fire. They would not have been able to touch you then. Remember, Earth stands. It is a good defence. Fire is mainly used for attack."

Malin was abashed. "I did not think of it. I am sorry, Master."

"Your use of Fire was good until you were angered. Anger is dangerous. You must not give in to it. You must learn to control it and use it to your advantage. In any combat, you must keep a cool head. Then you are in control. Once you learn control, your powers will be great."

Malin's face lightened.

"However -" continued the wizard.

The smile on the youth's face fell.

"You let your guard drop. It is not a good thing to do when enemies surround you." Goldwen punctuated this with a stern look.

"I - I - Thought that they - had - had -,"

"Killed me?" supplied Goldwen. "You should have thought of your own welfare. If you are to defend Erathyn and yourself, you must learn how to fight."

"I have not killed anything before. The Man's death was terrible."

Goldwen stroked his chin.

"You have not killed now," he said. "They were all an illusion."

Relief passed across the youth's face. He looked around and saw no evidence of the Men ever being there. Goldwen pointed at his wounded arm. There was not a mark on him!

"I do not like your tests," said Malin.

"I do not know anyone who likes tests," said Goldwen. "Come. Show me how to create a shield."

In the shadows of the forest, Brack sat back and smiled to himself. He had watched the scene of Malin and the Men, instantly realizing that it was all a test. He had seen all that had occurred, and he felt nothing but contempt for his brother. His *brother*. Malin had no idea of the powers that were awakening in him. He could not control them, and it was plain to Brack that he was unsure of himself. He looked out and watched as Goldwen showed Malin how to make a shield to defend against attacks.

"If you keep the shield in your mind as a wall of impenetrable rock, you cannot be harmed," said Goldwen. "Do it now."

Malin nodded and concentrated on what Goldwen had taught him.

The wizard took up his staff, and without warning, rushed at Malin and struck out at him. The blow never fell. With a flash, the staff rebounded from the shield. Malin winced at the stroke, but was relieved to find himself unharmed. Goldwen followed with a flurry of hits: the shield deflected all. He lowered his staff. "Good," he said.

Brack laughed to himself. If this was the best that Malin could do, he had no fears. He left them to play their games and slipped away to return to Algol, chuckling to himself.

Goldwen stood before Malin, and a smile came to his face. He had been aware of the unseen watcher's presence, and now felt Brack's departure. He said nothing to Malin about it. Let Brack be ignorant also of what he was now to show his pupil. "Now the shield is good against physical attack," he said, "But against a magical assault..." He thrust his arm forward, and his fingers flicked out at Malin. A blast of energy left Goldwen's hand, and Malin was thrown to the ground.

He looked up at the wizard in astonishment. The security he had felt from the shield evaporated. Goldwen came over and helped him rise.

"For defence against magic we use the Ten-fold Mirror," he said.

Malin shook his head. "The Ten-fold Mirror?" The boy echoed. "What is that?"

"Imagine a full-length mirror in front of you." Goldwen looked to see if Malin followed him. He did. "Then turn it around so that the reflective surface faces away from you. Now imagine others around you; on your right hand, your left, and behind you. That is four. Then one diagonally on your left between the one in front and the one on your left; one behind to the left, one forward and one rear to the right, and you have eight mirrors, all facing away from you. But I said Ten-fold did I not? Where would the other two be?" His gaze pierced the other, waiting for an answer. One eyebrow rose. "Well?"

Malin thought for a moment. Mirrors all around him. All around him... Where would the other two be? No! Not *all* around him. He wondered if it was the right answer. It *seemed* logical...

He looked at Goldwen. "Above and below?" He asked hopefully.

The wizard's smile grew radiant. He nodded vigorously. "Yes, my boy!" He said exultantly. "Very good. Now show me. Concentrate on the image of the mirrors."

Malin frowned. "But which element is used for the mirror?"

"Ah," replied the wizard, "It is the Five."

"The Five?"

Goldwen nodded. "The Five is all of the Elements used in conjunction."

"Why?"

"Think of it this way. We use Earth because a mirror is made from substances taken from it. Air because the reflection in it is as clear as the Air. Fire because a mirror is made from great heat. Water because the water is used to cool it down when the Fire has shaped it, and Void because when we turn it around, the reverse is darkness. The mirror formed of the Five is impossible to breach. The mirror will deflect any magical attack, returning the energy back to the attacker. Unlike the shield, the mirror cannot be penetrated. It is very important to have in your mind, ready to be conjured at all times."

Malin nodded. He conjured the image in his mind, seeing the Five as a great union of the elements, the mirror formed about him, encasing him in an impenetrable cocoon.

This time the attack was expected. But the energy was deflected as easily as the staff had been by the shield.

"Well done," said Goldwen. "It is a good idea to form the mirror in your mind as soon as you wake, and before you sleep. Make it a habit, and it may save your life. Do not forget the ones above and below. It is easy to do, because we do not think of being attacked from such directions, but such attacks are possible, especially against the unwary." He noted the satisfaction on his pupil's face. He was proud to have shown Goldwen that he could learn quickly. "Now," he continued, "Let us see about the other Elements. As you know how to defend yourself, let us now proceed to attack..."

It was late afternoon. The sun was going down, painting the region in ruddy tones as Malin and Goldwen walked down the road towards Algol. A large group of riders were approaching, coming down from the same direction as the road from Oakdean. The two stopped at the bridge and waited for them.

They were all clad in the forest green of the Elves, carrying the standard of the King. This was an eight pointed star, in silver, set upon a great forest oak in natural brown tones on a green background of many hues, which denoted the forest. The first half of the company rode armed with longknife and spear, and wore glittering helms and breastplates. The other half wore longknives and had Elven longbows with quivers of arrows slung across their backs. They too wore light helms, but had no armour. Two figures in the midst of the column stood out because of their finer dress and bearing.

One was a tall and commanding presence, his long blonde hair confined by a simple silver fillet. His riding clothes and his richly caparisoned mount proclaimed him the leader of the group. His face, open and pleasant, held knowledge and power. Also, one could sense that he weighed everything that he saw and heard with good judgement. As the pair watched, it was also apparent that he was possessed with a fine wit, for he and his companion and the leader of the riders laughed and joked as they approached. Their smiles flashed and the sound of their merriment rang clearly in the air. Yet there was the sensation that if there was need of immediate and decisive action, he would not be found wanting. He was truly a kingly figure amongst his noble escort.

"The King!" said Goldwen.

The column halted before them. King Anarys rode forward, accompanied by his two companions. Goldwen and Malin bowed respectfully as the riders reined in.

"Welcome to Algol, Sire," said Goldwen.

"Eldest," said the King, "I had not expected you to welcome me before the gates." Anarys saw that Goldwen was wearing a plain grey robe, not the robe of the Eldest. He was puzzled. What could this mean? His gaze strayed to Malin.

"I am afraid that title no longer refers to me, Your Majesty," returned the wizard. "I have stepped down to instruct my pupil." He indicated Malin beside him.

The King nodded and smiled at the youth. "Then you are one of the two who I have come to see." His eyes were a piercing blue, probing Malin's face.

Malin felt uncomfortable under the scrutiny of his stare. He bowed again, saying: "Thank you, - uh – Sire."

Anarys, seeing his discomfort, softened his gaze. He could sense no taint of Dark Magic about the youth. Surely Goldwen had been right in his decision to create him? He turned and introduced the two others who sat their mounts. "This is my daughter, the Princess Willowen."

For the first time Malin saw her, sitting with stately poise upon her horse. She was a vision of loveliness there in the sunset, tall and lithe. She wore a riding tunic like her father, not a gown, and her figure and limbs could be seen as clean and well formed. Her eyes shone an electric blue. Her hair, like her sire's, was a long golden dream, which flowed down her back. Her face held a beauty that seemed to put all of the Elven women he had seen to shame. It glowed with a vitality that showed through the clear skin. He thought she must be the most beautiful creature on the face of Erathyn. Then she smiled at him. He was overpowered and could only stand there with his mouth open.

"*Oh,*" he breathed.

The princess looked down at him, and her smile broadened as Malin dimly heard the King introduce the other Elven woman, who was dressed as the warriors were. There was something about the Captain of the Bowmays, and the princess's personal bodyguard. He paid no attention, drinking in Willowen's beauty. He heard Anarys falter to a stop, and then laughter brought him to himself. He blinked and looked around to see them all laughing. He blushed and bowed his head.

He felt Goldwen's hand on his shoulder and looked up. His face burned with shame. He had disgraced himself before the King and the Princess!

Willowen still smiled at him. There was no malice or mockery in her smile. The others also had no ridicule on their faces. He was astounded. Apart from Goldwen, the Elves of Algol were quite restrained and solemn. Obviously other Elves from outside the City of the Wizards were not the same.

"Do you have a name?" The musical tones came to his ear. The princess had spoken to him. The sound of her voice pleased the ear as much as her form the eye. Her own eyes glittered merrily at him.

"Malin, My Princess," he answered.

"Ah," said the King. "Was that your idea, Goldwen?" Mirth still showed on his face.

"No, Your Majesty." He smiled. "That is, I *suggested* it – but it was his own decision to accept that name." He was clearly proud of his pupil.

Anarys leaned forward on his horse. "Please forgive us, Malin," he said. "We did not mean to embarrass you." It was this attitude to respect those lower than him that the King was well known and loved for.

"I am sorry – Your Majesty," said Malin. "Forgive me, My Princess."

"There is nothing to forgive," she said in dulcet tones. "This must be all strange to you."

Malin could not think of a fitting reply. His short existence had been accelerated by the application of magic. Indeed, he had been created by it. How could he describe to them what he felt, or how he struggled to reconcile his very existence? And then there was the fact of his brother, and the thoughts of the Council.

"It is," was all he replied.

"Who is the Eldest then?" Inquired the King.

Goldwen's smile became wry. "Amberon is the Eldest."

Anarys considered this. "Well," he said, "he has wanted the position long enough. Now he has his wish."

"Let us hope that he is now satisfied that it is his. However, Sire, he has also raised Candreen to be the Master of Void magic. Along with his other allies, this means that he has complete control of all Council decisions."

"What of the other...child?"

"He calls himself Brack, Your Majesty," said Goldwen.

How appropriate, thought Anarys. "And the Council is absolutely certain about the Dark One's involvement?"

"Yes. Somehow he has freed himself from the Ice of Foreverness. I sent Vandaron to investigate after I suspected that it was Malkaar who had used his sorcery on the Lady Elinor. He said he saw a huge army, and fought the Dark One himself. There is no doubt that he has reappeared."

"I see," said the Elven-King. "And this Brack?"

"I believe that Malkaar has created him to revive the Black Circle. As you know, all of his followers were destroyed during the War. Also, it could be that in his own twisted way, he seeks to use the blood of the Elves in his revenge. Remember, Your Majesty, that we were his greatest enemies."

The King recalled those bitter days of conflict, when all of the races of Erathyn had stood to defy the dark ambitions of Malkaar. Many had fallen; Nerolynn his queen among them, and then the races had drifted apart. Even though they had been victorious, the ending of the Union of Races seemed to be the last malicious design of the Dark One. Men feared and distrusted the Elves; the Dwarves hid themselves in their mountain kingdom.

"Indeed," said Anarys. "We destroyed the Black Circle once before, it must not be allowed to rise again." The King thought for a moment. "And Lord Malor? How is he faring?"

"Elinor's death was very hard on him," said Goldwen. "But he has promised me that the folk of Oakendean will support us against Malkaar."

"And afterwards?"

"They will join us for the return to Glindarion. He and I are reconciled. Your command will be obeyed."

"Say not *command*, Goldwen. Rather it is my wish that the Elves should again become one. This world has brought much heartbreak to us. Let us not forget the many who have fallen. Erathyn's beauty has been spoiled by violence and war. It is not only the Dark One who is enamoured of power. Men desire it above all other things. Perhaps Lord Malor and his supporters are right: we should not have become involved in Men's affairs."

The wizard shook his head. "No, Sire. Men alone could not have fought Malkaar. You recall how difficult it was to persuade the Dwarves to help. They would have left Men to their fate. However, it was right that both we and the Dwarves helped them. This world would be now under the sorcerer's control if we had not been involved. If we had not brought the Felininn and Avianinn into the conflict, the world of Men would have fallen. Men would be his pitiful slaves, or they would be dead."

An uncomfortable silence fell, which was broken by the clear sound of trumpets ringing in the air. They all looked to the city, where they could see an honour guard lining the road, and standing in the gate, the Council, Amberon in its midst.

"Well," said the King, "We must not keep them waiting, hmm? I can sense Amberon's impatience from here." Some laughter followed this as Anarys told the leader to advance into the city. As they turned their mounts to return to their former position, the King spoke to Goldwen and Malin.

"When all of the formalities are done, we shall have a banquet in the great hall. We shall speak again and enjoy each other's company."

Princess Willowen smiled at Malin, saying; "I look forward to sitting and talking to you. I want to hear all about you."

Malin's eyes shone. She wanted to talk to him! He bowed low, not seeing the glance that Goldwen and Anarys shared. Then Goldwen and Malin stepped aside as the column reformed and rode forward. Malin noticed that the archers at the rear of the column were all women. He turned to Goldwen, who had anticipated his question.

"They are the bowmays. They are an elite company of archers led by Captain Nilda. All of them are excellent shots." He looked at them as they passed. He glanced at Malin, saying; "If you had been paying attention, instead of gaping at Princess Willowen, you would know all this." The smile on his face showed that he was teasing.

Malin had looked away from the bowmays and was following the upright figure riding next to King Anarys. She was magnificent. What could he talk about to her? As he watched, it was as though she heard his thoughts, for she looked over her shoulder and gave him a smile that pierced his heart. As she turned forward again, he blushed fiercely.

Goldwen observed all this, a wry smile on his face. He started to follow the procession, but stopped as he realised that Malin was not with him. He turned and saw the youth standing with a rapt smile on his face. Goldwen went back to him.

"*Beautiful,*" breathed the boy.

"You had better forget about her. You are to be a wizard trained in the Arts of High Magic, and you cannot waste your powers on a mere woman."

Malin looked at Goldwen with a puzzled look on his face. "*Mere* woman? She is the most *beautiful* woman I have ever seen."

Goldwen frowned at him admonishingly. "It is no good, Malin," said the wizard. "I know what is in your heart. I too had to forsake someone's love for the Arts."

The youth turned and stared at the column as the Council met it. It then entered the gates and was gone. His shoulders slumped. Goldwen took his arm, and they crossed the bridge and entered the gates in their turn.

Above, in the Tower of the Eldest, Brack had seen all of this, and he smiled to himself. *A Princess, hmm.*

The unseen presence of the Dark One hovered over him. He could feel the scrutiny of its will.

"Do you want her . . . ?"

The smile on Brack's lips became a predatory one. He nodded. "She is beautiful. But I suppose that she is like all the other Elven women. She would be no challenge."

"No . . . She is not . . . She is . . . different."

Brack's face became thoughtful. "*Different?* In what way?"

"She has powers unlike the others . . . I want you to bring her to me."

"When?"

"I will tell you . . . When I have finished with her, you may have her."

Brack thought of the beautiful face. He would like to see her as his slave. It appealed to his humour to think of her humbled before him. The other Elves of the city either ignored him or shunned him. This would show them not to treat him badly.

"It will be done," he said, bowing low as the force faded away.

CHAPTER VII

THE TESTING

The banquet hall in the Tower of Banadon was full of colour, music and polite conversation. The fair voices of the Elves hummed softly, occasionally rising in song and laughter. It was not the boisterous humour that one would expect from Men's tables; it was dignified and graceful. The atmosphere was one of refined elegance. In the soft golden light of candles, the host sat eating and drinking as the sweet sounds of harp and pipe echoed melodiously through the hall. The various colours of the robes and gowns moved and shifted as though a field of multi-hued flowers had entered the hall. Servants moved through the crowd with trays of food and drink.

The King's party and the Council of Light quaffed honey-wine and ate from the provender spread before them on the board at which they sat. King Anarys, Princess Willowen, and their entourage fell to with a will, for it was a long, hard journey from the King's high-seat in Melarion to Algol. They had changed out of their stained riding gear, and were now dressed in courtly finery. Even the King's escort and the bowmays were clothed in rainbow hues, where they sat at the lower tables.

Princess Willowen, clad now in a light blue silken gown, looked radiantly beautiful, and held the attention of many a glance from around the room. Her luxurious blonde hair fell down her back, glinting in the glow of the candlelight. On her snow-white breast a pendant with a green stone hung, reflecting the light as she turned and moved. She was a delight to watch as she ate daintily from the plate before her. Every now and then, her fine hands would take up her goblet and raise it to her lips. She listened to the music with pleasure, for music was something that she loved. Anarys caught her eye and they both shared a smile. He raised his goblet to her and she did the same in return, laughing.

King Anarys was seated in the centre of this gathering, the rightful place for a visiting monarch. The Eldest sat to his right hand, Willowen to his left, and the members of the Council were seated on either side of the King as befitted their station. Behind him to his right stood a young pageboy with the King's own crystal wine flagon.

Anarys sat upon his throne in a relaxed manner, joining in conversation from time to time. Occasionally, he would look around the hall at his people. His gaze became thoughtful as he recalled the many Elves who had fallen in the War of the Races. He stared at the ring on his left hand: a gift from his wife, gone these many years. She had supported him unflinchingly when he had organised the Union of Races Her fall at the last battle haunted him still.

Anarys cast his mind back to that fateful day. He remembered how they had parted; he and Goldwen had taken the High Pass, and Nerolynn had gone with the other force. Goldwen had assured him that Paranon was as powerful a wizard as himself, and that he shouldn't worry about Nerolynn's safety. Anarys had instructed Paranon to keep the Queen safe. She had laughed, and told him that she would take care. Nerolynn had kissed him, and her smile had remained with him as she had turned and led her warriors away. Anarys and his own force had marched into the High Pass, intending to take Malkaar by surprise, but it was they who were ambushed. The Dark One had been waiting for them, and he and Goldwen fought with magical forces as Anarys and the warriors engaged the Cobrans who had accompanied Malkaar. Then - the mountain had fallen down upon them, and Anarys had known no more until Goldwen had managed to revive him.

He took a long drink from his goblet, drained it, and put it down on the board in front of him. He stared at the food before him, and felt his appetite drain away. He continued to stare as the young page at his back hurried forward, refilled his goblet, bowed, and returned to his position.

Anarys thought of the last time that he had seen Nerolynn. After they had recovered all those who had survived the fall of rock, they had left a group of warriors to gather up the dead, and made their way down to Malkaar's tower. In the valley they had come upon the two armies, held in thrall by the Spell of Stasis. After a long search, the Queen had been found, frozen into immobility like all the rest. No matter what he had tried, Goldwen could not negate the spell. He had attempted to break the spell with every counterspell he knew, working tirelessly for hours as the King had looked on in despair. Several of the King's warriors had returned after going forward and checking the battlefield. They reported that the Dark One's tower was held fast by layers of impenetrable ice, and Anarys and Goldwen realised that Shaarla had been successful. As the night began to fall, Goldwen had admitted that he could not break the spell, and they had gathered the remnants of the Army of Light, and begun the long march home, leaving Nerolynn and their comrades trapped in Malkaar's spell. That had been almost a thousand years ago. Goldwen had returned many times to try to break the spell, using new knowledge that he had learned, but nothing had worked. Nerolynn and the two armies remained where they were, still and silent.

He looked up and turned to stare at his daughter. She was the only reminder of his queen, a mirror image of how Nerolynn had looked in her youth. He must not lose her as well. Willowen felt the intensity of his stare and returned his gaze. She realised that he was lost in memory, and smiled. He caught the smile, and came out of his reverie and returned it sadly. She reached over and took his hand. He placed his other hand over hers, and Willowen leaned towards him and kissed him on the cheek. Anarys took up his goblet and offered it to her. The Princess took the goblet, and rose to her feet.

"All hail the King!" she cried.

Everyone in the hall rose to their feet, and held their goblets aloft.

"All hail the King!"

Anarys gestured for the throng to return to their seats. Willowen sat down, and gave him his goblet. He held it out to her.

"I only meant for you to take a drink, daughter. I did not want a salutation from my subjects. I know that they respect me."

"I know, Father." She accepted the goblet, and drank from it. She handed it back to him. "They respect and love you, Father. As do I."

The King smiled, and this time there was no sadness in it.

"And I love you." Anarys stroked her cheek affectionately.

Captain Nilda, in her position as bodyguard to Willowen, sat on her left. Korwen was attempting to engage her in conversation, but she only replied to him to be polite. She was looking around the hall for this Brack. A sense of unease had entered her heart when they had come to the city. From time to time, she would glance at Willowen and the resolve to protect the Princess with her own life would rise in her breast. Korwen's words fell on deaf ears. Nilda watched as the figure of Candreen entered the hall and crossed the floor. He bowed before the King and came around the table to whisper in the Eldest's ear. Amberon's face grew hard as he listened. Anarys watched silently.

He listened intently, but the conversation was pitched too low for him to hear. The fact that Goldwen had stepped down to make Amberon the Eldest concerned him greatly. Many times in the past, Amberon had shown himself to be self-seeking. Not quite the type to be the head of the Council. Still, Goldwen had proven to be a good servant of the King, and also of Erathyn. His reputation was impeccable, and of all the Elves, he was the only one that was highly thought of by the other races. Surely his judgement in this matter could be trusted?

Servants moved through the throng, distributing honey-wine and sweetmeats to the guests. The hall had a dream-like atmosphere, as when one drinks in a heated room, and feels oneself starting to drowse. The warmth of the evening and the wine raised the spirits of all in the hall. The Elven musicians played on as the feasters enjoyed themselves.

The King's gaze had travelled each table in the hall. He was pleased that his subjects were in good cheer. However, after taking in the sight, he recalled what he had come to see. He leaned back in his throne and spoke without raising his voice: "Eldest."

The Eldest, who had been talking to Candreen, turned. "Majesty?"

"Where is Goldwen?"

Anarys drained his goblet and gestured over his shoulder. The young page hurried forward with his flagon and refilled it. Meanwhile the King's level stare stayed on Amberon. Nearby feasters sensed a moment of confrontation; conversation ebbed and even the music faded. Candreen straightened from where he had been stooping at the Eldest's side. A few last notes from the harp died into the stillness.

Amberon bowed his head. "I must apologize, Sire. Goldwen -"

"- is here," said Goldwen, bowing before the King. "Your servant, as ever, Majesty."

Beside him, Malin also bowed, but only after gazing at Willowen, who smiled at him.

"Ah," said Anarys, "I see that you are still disrespectful of authority." A wry smile and a twinkle in his eyes belied the rebuke.

"No disrespect was intended, Sire. I was merely ensuring that Malin was sure of how to conduct himself in your august presence." Goldwen placed his hand on Malin's shoulder and motioned him forward.

The youth knelt in the finest manner of the court, saying; "My heart and hands are yours, My Liege."

This widened the smile on the King's face. He turned to the Eldest.

"And where is your protégé, Eldest?"

Amberon gritted his teeth in a smile that barely concealed his anger. He scowled at Goldwen and his charge. The atmosphere in the hall became tense. Goldwen addressed himself to the Eldest.

"Will you not answer your king, Eldest?"

Amberon's eyes slitted as he glared at Goldwen. As he faced the King, he forced his gaze to be milder. All there could see the effort that this took. His manner became apologetic. Candreen made as if to speak, but Goldwen's eyes burned into him, and he was cowed and stilled. He stood silently by Amberon's chair as the Eldest spoke.

"Majesty -" Amberon began.

"Yes?" said the King.

Amberon's discomfiture was obvious. Suddenly a powerful cold presence was felt in the hall. The candles guttered and the light dimmed. The warmth drained from the room. The main doors swung open of their own accord, and a figure strode in. The doors crashed together again, the only sound in the hush which had fallen over the chamber. The attention of all was turned to the doors, where there stood a tall Elf, dressed in finery to match the King's. In the dulled candlelight, the red of his clothing seemed to be as dark as blood.

"I believe that His Majesty wishes to see me?" He did not raise his voice, but the words were carried throughout the hall in ringing tones. Brack entered the room, and as he did so, the warmth returned. The candles flared brightly for a moment, then returned to their normal glow. All eyes remained on him as he crossed the floor to stand before the King, where he bowed elaborately. As he stood, his night-dark eyes met those of Amberon, and he smiled as the Eldest's lips turned down in irritation. He turned to stare at Willowen, drinking in her beautiful face, and the golden blonde of her long hair. He bowed again, this time to her, but his eyes left her face and travelled down her throat to her breast. He smiled lecherously.

"My lady."

A dark blush flowered in her cheeks and she turned away from him as if angry and affronted. There was no way that his gaze could be mistaken for that of a respectful subject. By her side, Nilda's angry stare was completely ignored by Brack.

He came forward to take up Willowen's goblet, but he snatched his hand back just in time as Nilda's dagger flashed down and thudded deeply into the table top. The captain of the bowmays wrenched it out of the board and stood with it extended towards him. *"You dare!"* She cried. Her eyes flamed, and if the table had not been between them, she would have thrown herself upon him.

A few gasps of shock and outrage pierced the silence. Several of the King's escorts and the bowmays rose swiftly at their captain's action. Malin made as if to move to confront Brack, but Goldwen caught his arm and held him fast.

The shock of the sudden attack had made Brack leap backwards. The fire in Nilda's eyes cut through his superior poise. To cover his discomfort, he laughed in derision and stood with his fists on his hips, his feet spread wide.

Willowen leapt to her feet and caught Nilda's arm in a vice-like grip. She forced the captain's arm down slowly. Nilda glared at Brack, and then turned to her mistress, who shook her head. The captain returned her weapon to its sheath, her eyes never leaving Brack's face. She sat down, but looked as though she would leap to Willowen's defence in an instant.

"A faithful servant!" Sneered Brack mockingly. He bowed to Nilda, who returned his look scornfully. The host remained in shocked silence.

Anarys had watched Nilda's actions with appreciation. He had assigned her as bodyguard to his daughter himself. Willowen was prone to be headstrong, and he felt better that Nilda was there to keep an eye on her. Now he spoke to Brack.

"Well, I imagine the captain does not wish you to share her lady's drink. Perhaps you should have your own?"

Brack smiled. "An excellent idea, Your Majesty." He snapped his fingers, and with a bright flash a goblet appeared and hovered in the air before him. He reached out and took it. Bringing it to his lips, he drank deeply. Brack lowered the goblet, and regarded the group seated before him with a silken smile.

"It seems you have a good grasp of the principles of magic," Anarys said.

"Thank you, Sire." He bowed. Brack saw that his little display had impressed the Councillors. He was satisfied that they were aware of his power.

Anarys made a gesture of welcome to the newcomers, indicating the table. "Please join us."

Brack's gaze travelled the length of the table, taking in the King, the Princess and Nilda, and the Eldest and the Council. He turned and considered Goldwen and his useless brother, and smiled to himself. There were none here that could stand against him. Let them all think that they were powerful. He would show them. The room waited expectantly for his reply.

The tension in the hall hung for a moment longer, and then Brack nodded to Anarys. "Thank you, Your Majesty," he said with a smile.

He, Malin and Goldwen came forward to join the banquet. The three new arrivals were found seats at Willowen's end of the King's own table, Brack and Malin side by side at the very end of the board and Goldwen between Malin and the nearest Councillor. The guards and bowmays who had risen from their seats sat down again as the tension broke. Then in the body of the hall the musicians struck up, and gradually conversation grew animated again.

At the high table, all waited on the King's next words. The Eldest sat fidgeting, for he did not relish being shown for a fool, and he had no way of knowing what Brack would choose to say or do. His advisor stood behind him and glared at the three who had just sat down. He realised that here there was danger: to his master, and also to himself.

Anarys leaned forward to address the newcomers. "So," he said, "Here are the two miracles of which we have heard. I have come to see them for myself, and to preside over their testing."

At this, there were exclamations of shock from the Council members. Goldwen smiled and bowed to the King, as though he already knew what Anarys had had in mind. The King returned the smile and raised his goblet to his lips. Malin looked at Goldwen in alarm, but the wizard merely gripped his arm and nodded in a reassuring manner. Brack leaned back in his chair and smiled to himself. The Eldest turned to the King.

"Majesty," he began, "This is without precedence. These youths have not been fully trained."

"I know," replied Anarys. "The entire situation is unique. However, I believe that Goldwen has been teaching his charge, and your protégé has just demonstrated his knowledge of the Arts."

Brack acknowledged the King's praise with a small bow and a sardonic smile. The Eldest averted his eyes and stared at the board in front of him. His thoughts roiled in his brain. Finally, he raised his eyes to Anarys. His lips twisted a little as he smiled in submission. Anarys was well known for his stubbornness. The Eldest placed his hand upon his heart and bowed to his liege.

"If it is your will, Sire, then it shall be done." He thought of the Council, and of how they had made him Eldest; his dearest wish, but in the presence of the King, he was powerless. As he resignedly dropped his hand beside his plate, Anarys placed his hand over it.

"It is my will," he said firmly.

In the morning two very distinct groups gathered outside the Tower of Banadon to attend the ritual ceremony where the two youths would be tested on their grasp of their knowledge of the Arts. This would take place in the Tower of Sh'kaarl, which was in a part of the city that was far away from all of the other towers and buildings, and had for many years been traditionally used for just such a purpose. The two candidates would first be tested by a panel of judges that were made up of the members of the Council, answering questions and being interviewed on the theory of magic. After this, they would be given several 'problems' that they would have to demonstrate their practical skills with. Finally, they would enter the lowest regions of the tower to undergo the Ordeal to see if they could use such skills under stress. In the past, some candidates had died.

The King, the Princess, the Eldest, and the Councillors stood in a frigid wind that whipped their cloaks and hair around. The chill gusts had arrived early in the morning, as though they were emphasising the gravity of the day's events to come. Standing apart from them were the two candidates, Malin and Brack. They were dressed in the dull grey robes of candidates, and also wore grey belts, signifying their lowly status. Goldwen was to serve as Malin's attendant, and Candreen as Brack's. The two youths felt isolated from their judges, and glanced from time to time at the other group, wondering what they would have to face. This was a deliberate and psychological separation, designed to make the candidates uncomfortable. The Testing had already begun, although Malin and Brack were unaware of that fact.

Anarys, Willowen and the Eldest set off with the Councillors, well ahead of the other four. The Tower of Sh'kaarl was a short walk away; however, in the wind, it was most unpleasant as they strode along. The smaller group seemed to disintegrate as they followed. Though Malin stuck close to Goldwen's side, filled with trepidation, Brack drifted indifferently just ahead to their left, and Candreen was three strides behind the others, as though he held back. Malin paid no attention to the buffeting wind, but to him, the walk seemed to last for an eternity. Goldwen noticed his worried face and placed his arm around Malin's shoulders.

"Do you think I will do well?" said Malin pensively.

"You will be fine. Remember what I have taught you, and let your heart be your guide. The first thought you are given is the truth. Trust it."

Malin swallowed nervously, and then nodded. If Goldwen had confidence in his abilities, then he must think that he was ready. He turned to his left, where Brack was walking along, and saw the look of supreme confidence on his face. Brack felt his scrutiny and turned with a supercilious smile. Malin looked away.

The group hurried through the bitter wind towards the brother's rendezvous with destiny. No one spoke, for the wind now increased in intensity, blowing leaves and dust around the walkers. The other inhabitants of the city were nowhere to be seen, and all of the doors were shut against the onslaught that was but the beginning of a terrific storm, the dark and swollen clouds of which could be seen approaching from the East.

At last they arrived at the Tower of Sh'kaarl. Their judges were already somewhere within. It was a forbidding looking structure, made of a red-black stone called *nightblood,* which glistened wetly in the storm cloud's half-light. Now, as lightning flashed, it appeared to soak up the discharges as they flickered on the horizon. Thunder rolled deeply across the fields and echoed in the streets of the city.

The great door in the front of the tower was embossed with the symbols of all the elements; Earth, Air, Fire, Water, Void, which were depicted in a circular design. The dark Void was depicted by a black circle in the centre; a mound of soil representing Earth beneath it and the flame of Fire above it, while to the left was the cloud standing for Air and to the right the wave that represented Water.

Princess Willowen stepped forwards. In a ringing voice, she cried: "Guardian, by the pact we share, I summon you to test these candidates who we bring before you! Come forth!"

The symbols glowed, and a deep humming came from the door. A bright flash of light burst from the portal's centre, and Malin and Brack were blinded for a moment. The others, who knew what to expect, had looked downwards, avoiding the brilliance that rayed outwards. The glare faded, and the two youths looked in amazement at what was revealed before them.

Before the tower's single door stood a huge figure, half again as tall as the tallest of the group, wrapped completely in a brown robe and hood so that nothing of his face or hands could be seen. This was the Guardian of the tower who opened the door and led the party inside the darkened doorway without a word. He only bowed to them, and stooped under the doorframe as they followed him inside. The door closed, leaving the violence of the storm outside.

Opposite the external door were two arches, one with stairs leading up towards yellow torchlight (there was no other light-source in the room), and the other with damp, uneven steps leading down into darkness. The Guardian stood between the archways in ominous silence, his arms folded. Anarys ascended the stairs, and the Councillors climbed after him. Amberon gestured at the door, and it opened. The King entered, and the Councillors followed him into the room. The door closed.

Goldwen cleared his throat. "The Eldest will inform us in my mind when Malin is summoned. He will speak in Master Candreen's mind when Brack is summoned. Correct, Master Candreen?"

"Correct, Eld -, I mean, Master Goldwen."

Both candidates looked around as their eyes adjusted to the gloom, but the dark chamber had nothing to fix the mind on. Its walls were quite bare, undressed and unadorned stone, without even a stick of furniture or a fire to cheer. This was another psychological effect to make candidates uneasy before the real testing to come.

After a few minutes, Brack caught Malin's eye and said; "I hope you are not frightened, my brother." He had such a look on his face as one would give to a troubled child.

Malin did not answer.

Brack smiled to himself as he noted Malin's discomfort. He began to pace about the room. Malin watched him for a moment, and then looked away. The thunder reached them dimly through the walls. Goldwen, Willowen and Candreen stood as silently as the Guardian did.

Like a stalking animal, Brack paced the floor for what seemed an age

Brack walked up to the Guardian and addressed him, saying; "Will this take long?" He was trying to cover his own discomfort with a brash show of confidence.

The Guardian ignored him, motionless as a statue.

Brack started to become angry, and spoke again, saying; "I do not care for this. I shall leave." He turned from the Guardian and walked toward the door.

The Princess and Goldwen shared a knowing look.

The Guardian's right arm came up and his hand opened palm upward and he extended his arm after the retreating figure, then he clenched his fist and drew his arm back until it reached his chest. The hand now revealed was dark brown like the earth beneath their feet, with a golden light that seemed to emanate from within.

As he did this Brack stopped, and with a look of shock on his face, turned and walked back to the silent giant. Brack's face was sweaty, and he breathed in short gasps, as though he did this against his will. This was perfectly true. The others in the room watched this struggle between the Guardian and the haughty Elf. Goldwen smiled at Brack's surprise at being bested. Malin was amazed to see Brack so humbled before them. Candreen stood silently, a smirk of satisfaction on his face. Willowen smiled to herself, pleased that Brack had been put in his place.

The Guardian looked down at Brack and shook his head. His voice rumbled out for the first time, sounding like rocks grinding together: "You shall stay." The deep bass tones vibrated in their bones and echoed in the chamber. Brack's dark eyes tried to pierce beneath the hood but could see nothing of the face hidden in its shadow. He peered up at the towering shape; awed by such tremendous power in someone he had taken to be a mere servant. The giant figure grabbed the Elf by the shoulder, and marched him into the centre of the room. "Do not move," the hulking shape warned, and then strode back to stand between the doors.

Silence fell in the chamber. Both Malin and Brack regarded the Guardian with fearful looks. Brack remained where he had been placed, unwilling to risk another humilating encounter.

Candreen spoke, his voice sounding surprisingly loud in the uncomfortable silence that had fallen after Brack's embarrassing exploit: "Would candidate Brack please ascend the stairs for the first stage of his testing?"

Brack started, as if he had forgotten there were others in the room to witness his humiliation. He glared at them, hating that they should have seen his shameful defeat. He glanced nervously at the giant figure. Then he brushed past that massive form, as close to the wall as he possibly could, and surged impatiently up the stairs. Candreen followed, with a smile at his discomfort. He was pleased that the youth had been taken down a peg or two. As they neared the torches at the curve of the stairs, their shadows darkened all the room below.

Malin stood in the centre of the room, and gazed at Goldwen, at the stairs, and at the Guardian. Nothing changed however much he wished that it would. He thought he could hear something; a soft sound that was very low, and listened to try and make out what the sound was. Eventually, he realised that he he could hear soft chuckling. Malin looked over at where Goldwen stood. Goldwen was laughing quietly to himself.

"I bet that was a shock for the young upstart." He grinned.

Willowen smiled. "Yes," she said. "He did not expect that."

Malin's mouth dropped open as the Guardian came forward, saying; "Now, now, Your Highness, Master Goldwen, the youth was disrespectful."

Goldwen nodded. "Indeed, old friend. He needs to be kept in check."

"It was good to see him put in his place," Willowen said.

"There is Darkness in that one, Master Goldwen. Why has the Council agreed to test this youth? Why have you stepped down, and allowed Master Amberon to become Eldest? You know that he is not meant to lead the Council. Tell me why you have done these things."

Goldwen thought for a moment, and then he answered: "There is a much greater danger than Amberon or Brack. The Dark One has somehow escaped, and is amassing an army. He created Brack; for what reason, I am not certain. But I believe he created the boy to help him to revive the Black Circle." He indicated Malin. "I used his own sorcery to create Malin here, for I sensed that I was not powerful enough to face both the Dark One and his creation together."

"Was this a wise thing to do, Master Goldwen?" rumbled the giant figure. "The sorcery of the Black Circle is not to be trifled with. If the Dark One was responsible for the creation of these youths, then why were they not slain?" The cowl turned towards Malin, who froze in fear.

"You are not listening," Goldwen said. "*I* created Malin. There is no evil in him. I have given him much of my power."

"Can you be sure he is not evil?" Malin could feel the intensity of the Guardian's scrutiny.

"I am certain of it," Willowen said.

"See for yourself." Goldwen said.

Malin's terror grew as the Guardian came over to him. A massive hand descended to his shoulder and he felt the searching gaze of the Guardian fall upon him. It was as if the huge figure was peering deep within him. For a long moment there was silence, and then the giant figure spoke again.

"There is no taint of Darkness about you, young one. I can sense much power in you, but it is of Good, not Evil. Master Goldwen has made the right decision." The giant's hand left Malin and came to rest above the Guardian's heart. To the youth's growing wonder, the great form bowed deeply to him. "The forces of the Elementals shall serve you well."

Malin bowed in return, saying; "I - I thank you, Guardian." Malin took a deep breath. He realised he had been holding it.

"But this other youth has Darkness in him, Master Goldwen." The Guardian turned to the wizard. "It was a mistake to bring him here."

"We could not just test Malin, and not Brack," the wizard replied. "Amberon was adamant that both of them should face the test together." He gave the giant form a knowing look. "He could fail. Perhaps he could even *die*."

"I know what it is that you are asking of me," the Guardian replied, his voice grating like rocks, "but I cannot interfere in this matter. I cannot slay him out of hand. The Balance must be served." He paused for a moment, and then said: "But I can make the Ordeal - *difficult* for him." Somehow, Malin thought that the words held a smile behind them.

Goldwen did smile. "Then let us hope that it proves *too* difficult for him."

"Perhaps," the Guardian said. He returned his attention to Malin. "You too must face the Ordeal, young one. Do you believe you are ready?"

"I do not know," Malin answered truthfully. "But I will do my very best. I owe all to my master." He indicated Goldwen who inclined his head in acknowledgement. "It is because of his training and belief in me that I am being tested."

"This first part is easy, my boy," said the wizard.

"I hope so," said Malin, "I do not want to let you down."

"You will not fail," The Princess said. "I have complete faith in you." She gave him an encouraging smile.

Malin reddened. "I hope I can be worthy of your faith."

Goldwen nodded and stroked his chin.

"The oral examination is only a formality. You and Brack are obviously both gifted in the Arts. The 'problem' that you will be given will also be quite simple. But the Ordeal is a very strenuous and dangerous test." Here Goldwen looked at the Guardian. The tall figure nodded its head in confirmation of his words. "Remember that all is not what it seems," Goldwen said.

At this, the tall figure chuckled in a rich baritone, which somehow removed a little of Malin's fear. Then Brack and Candreen came down the stairs. Brack bowed sarcastically before Malin, saying; "Your turn, brother."

The smug look on his face turned to one of uneasiness as he saw the Guardian. Malin took what satisfaction he could from that as Goldwen said formally; "Would candidate Malin please ascend the stairs for the first stage of his testing?"

"Good luck," Willowen said.

The youth took what consolation he could from her words.

Malin and Goldwen climbed the stairs, passing two torches in stone sconces above the curve of the stairs. They stopped on a landing before the closed door.

"*Courage,*" whispered the wizard. He raised his right hand, and as he did, the door opened, seemingly of its own accord.

The King sat in the middle of the one table that was in the room with the Eldest and the Councillors arranged about him. Anarys beckoned to Malin, who strode forward and stopped before him. Goldwen entered the room after him, and the door closed behind him.

In the dark room below, Brack waited beside Candreen and the uncommunicative Guardian in stubborn silence as they waited for the next summons. Time stretched interminably. Finally Candreen spoke, as serenely as ever, "Would candidate Brack please ascend the stairs for the last stage of his testing?"

Brack and Candreen climbed the stairs again and came before the door, which opened when Candreen raised his right hand. Brack came forward at the King's gesture, and Candreen entered and stood beside Goldwen. They watched Brack strike a coolly superior pose beside his brother, who stood rigid, expectant and a little scared before the table. Goldwen smiled to himself as he remembered his own testing. Which stance, Goldwen wondered, hid the more trepidation?

The Eldest spoke for the Council, addressing them both. "You have both shown that you have a fine grasp of the Arts. The theory and practise of magic has been ably demonstrated in the 'problems' that you have each succeeded in." Here the Eldest paused. He looked intently at the pair. As usual, Brack had about him a superior air, but Malin was openly nervous. The Eldest continued; "Now you must undergo the Ordeal. If you are successful, and survive it, you will have passed the test and will be acknowledged as full wizards, and as such you will choose a Name of Power, leaving behind your former identity." He bowed to the King. "Your Majesty."

At this, Malin licked his lips and swallowed nervously, but Brack smiled to himself. He thought that all of this was a waste of time, but he would humour the King and his lackeys. The Eldest, he knew, was no challenge for him.

Anarys rose from his seat. "Thank you, Eldest," he said solemnly. "Candidates, if you are successful you will be accepted as wizards before this Council and in my sight. The innate grasp that you both have of the magical Arts will be put to the test in the Ordeal, where you will show the mastery and skills that a wizard requires. The fact that you both have needed hardly any teaching is remarkable. You are both born of magic, and your destinies are inextricably entwined with it."

He raised his sceptre. "Take their belts of candidature," he commanded, and the attendants came forward. Brack unwound and dropped his belt for Candreen to pick up, but Malin courteously handed his to Goldwen. "For now," the King said gravely, "they are no longer candidates but wizards or outcasts." He struck the floor with the heel of his sceptre.

The door opened and the Guardian entered. He crossed the floor and bowed before them. The King addressed the Guardian.

"Guardian, so that magic may be furthered in our realm, we deliver these candidates to you to face the Ordeal." He indicated Malin and Brack in turn with his sceptre. The Guardian bowed, came forward, and took Malin's left arm in one broad hand and Brack's right arm in the other, and led them unresisting from the room and down the stairs. Brack stared straight ahead; Malin stole one glance back at Goldwen, the fear written clearly in his face.

"*Remember*," mouthed the wizard just before the door closed.

In the gloomy downstairs chamber where the candidates had stood, the Guardian released Brack's arm, and in his booming voice told him; "Wait." He guided Malin into that other archway, where broken steps glistening with cold ooze led down into total darkness.

Willowen gave him a smile that was meant to lift his spirits, but Malin felt that his heart was plunging into his boots. He gazed at her, his face blank with fear. As the Guardian's huge hand impelled him forwards, Malin turned and stared at the yawning doorway before him and wondered what awful trial he was going to face. The Elf stepped over the threshold, and began the long descent into darkness. The Guardian's heavy footfalls sounded larger still in the confined space as the giant figure followed him downwards.

Down and down they went, seemingly into the bowels of the world. As they descended the treacherous steps, the only light came from the ooze, which coated the walls, a green glow which dimly illuminated the passage. The Elf sweated freely in his fear, his imagination conjuring numerous nightmare forms that rushed to meet him. His heart pounded, and he wished for the whole experience to end. He had no idea what he would be faced with, and his fevered mind continued to throw visions of unknown terrors before his eyes. Their footsteps seemed to grow louder and louder as he and his escort descended the interminable tunnel, matching time with his racing heart. A musty smell assailed his nostrils, and he coughed as it invaded his labouring lungs.

The steps ended. They were in a large, cave-like space, which shone with a faint greenish light, as the stairway had done. There was nothing in this cavern: no furniture, tapestries, or anything to break the monotony of the surrounding rock.

The Guardian propelled Malin to the centre of the room and stood behind him with his arms folded. The glow vanished to be replaced with a blackness that was almost palpable. Malin gasped, taken by surprise.

At that moment, the wall before him seemed to light up, dazzling him with its brilliance, as cracks formed on its surface. The light raced around the cave and surrounded him. The walls were closing in on him!

The formerly hard and immovable walls contracted around him at nightmare speed, until he thought he would be crushed within their deadly embrace. Frantically, he cast several spells to halt their progress, but to no avail. He turned to seek the Guardian, but his silent companion had vanished, leaving him to face the Ordeal alone. Malin hadn't even noticed his departure.

Then, he thought of Goldwen's advice, and almost seemed to hear the wizard's voice.

"Remember that all is not what it seems."

He closed his eyes and waited. The sweat ran down his trembling form as he listened, waiting to feel the rocks close around his body. Moments passed and nothing happened. He opened his eyes, and the cavern was as it had been when he had entered it. An illusion.

At this, a shrieking wind struck him full in the face, whipping his robe around him, and pushing him backwards. This was no illusion. He must disperse the wind. He cast into his mind for the spell as he was spun and tossed by the roaring storm of air, slamming against the walls painfully.

He had it! Malin spoke a Word of Command, and instantly he was dropped to the floor as the punishing winds shut off with a clap of thunder. He picked himself up, seeing that his robe was torn in several places and a few minor cuts on his hands and face had mixed their blood with his sweat.

From out of the walls shot great tongues of flame, billowing inwards toward him, their blistering heat scorching his skin. *Fire*, he thought, *that would follow the Elements in series.*

This time, the spell came to him easily. As he spoke it, the flames were snuffed out, leaving the cave hot and baking. Malin wracked his brain to try and anticipate the next trial. *Earth, Air, Fire* - he thought desperately.

Smashing down on him in great torrents from all directions came...

"Water!" spluttered Malin, fighting to keep upright in the deluge. The cavern quickly became waist deep with the rushing torrent, spinning and rising higher toward the ceiling. He sought desperately for the spell to nullify the swirling flood.

Then he found it. He cried out the Word of Command. The rushing water ceased, leaving the cavern wet and uncomfortable, and Malin stood in the dripping rags that had been his robe. The water ran down the walls, the walls that had undergone so many changes within moments.

Then - The Void! The cave was suddenly as dark as it had been before, but this time, there was no air. Malin suddenly gasped for the life-giving stuff, but nothing happened. The blood in his ears pounded savagely, and his heart and lungs worked vainly for relief as he strove to breathe. He slumped to the floor as the oxygen in his lungs began to give out. Spots of colour danced before his darkening vision and his hands clenched in the mud of the floor as he struggled to breathe.

Into his dimming thoughts came the terrible thought that here he was finished after all, and he could feel his body slipping into death.

Air, he thought, *Must...have...Air!*

Suddenly he knew. It must be Summoning this time, not Abjurgation. The spell left his blue lips. Instantly, air rushed into the killing vacuum of the Void, and he dragged deep lung-filling breaths, shuddering on the floor as he returned to life, like a newborn babe. Worn out by his trials, he fell into blackness.

The green glow returned, and with it came the Guardian, who bent and picked Malin up as though he were a child. The pair left the terrible cave behind and ascended the stairs. Malin was vaguely aware of this, but he watched their progress as if he were in a dream; he could scarcely feel the Guardian's arms around him. They traversed the endless steps much faster than they had descended them. They passed the figure of Brack, whose confident demeanour vanished as he saw the state of his brother. The giant carried Malin up into the entryway of the tower, and out of the door, where the King, the Princess, the Eldest, the Councillors and Goldwen and Candreen waited. There, the silent figure laid him on the grass, and bowing before them, said: "Now for the confident one." The entire group smiled at this, and the Guardian withdrew into the tower.

The storm had passed, and the sunshine revived Malin, who looked up and around, half expecting to see the dark confines of the cave. As he saw the group, he made to kneel before the King. Anarys reached down and raised him to stand before him.

"Congratulations," he said, "Your Ordeal is over."

Malin looked at him in surprise, and then stammered, "Majesty?"

The Eldest and the Council placed their left hands over their hearts and extended their right hands, palms up. "Welcome, Brother!" they chorused.

Malin stared at the group in wonder, and then turned to Goldwen.

The wizard bowed and made the same gesture as the Councillors, and then he winked at Malin.

Willowen's smile was broad. "I told you you would be successful."

Malin's heart soared. He was a wizard!

The Guardian reached Brack and gripped his arm firmly. Then they followed the steps down into the green-flecked darkness as Malin had done. When they reached the cave, the Guardian pushed Brack into the centre of the floor. Brack stumbled and turned to glare at the giant, but he had vanished. The Elf scanned the cavern in amazement. The blackness suddenly cut off his sight, and he cried aloud at the darkness. Suddenly, a rush of water smashed him to his knees, as it poured into the cave.

"Master!" he cried. The presence of the Dark One could not be felt. For the first time, he was truly alone. He would be forced to rely on his own strength. In front of the others, especially his brother, he appeared supremely confident, but that was only outward show. Without the Dark One's help, could he even stay alive? The rushing waters filled the cavern, and he rose swiftly to the top of them, buffeted by the waves. He thought desperately for a spell to nullify the flood.

"Your Master cannot hear you now. Survive if you can." The sepulchral tones tolled in his head like a great bell. The Guardian was content to kill him!

Finally he spoke a Word of Power. The waters ceased abruptly, and he fell from the roof and crashed to the floor painfully. As he rose to his knees, a howling wind threw him against the wall, shrieking and tearing at him. He gasped for breath, searching his numbing brain for the counter-spell. He found it and cried out the spell. The wailing tempest shut off with a clap of thunder, and he sagged to the floor.

He heard a cracking sound, and looking up, he saw in horror that long spears of stone were forming out of the living rock and extending themselves towards him. He leapt to his feet just in time to dodge the first one as it smashed into the wall. Then a macabre dance of death ensued as he frantically tried to avoid the plunging spears of rock that sought his life. Surely his brother had not faced such an assault. He began to think that the Guardian had treated Malin more fairly. As he dodged and ran around the cave, he roared in anger at the unfairness of it all.

Then he remembered a spell and used it. The thrusting spears vanished into the walls, and he bent double, drawing in racking breaths. His heart thundered in his chest, and his lungs laboured after his exertions.

The Void came. The life-giving air vanished from the cave. He fell to the muddy floor, gasping like a landed fish as he writhed and strove to breathe. His vision reddened as he began to black out. All at once, he realised that he had to Summon air. It was the exact opposite to his responses so far. As he panted out the spell, and the air rushed back into the cavern and into his overworking lungs, he wept in relief.

Flames rushed out of the walls towards him. Instinctively, he threw his hands in front of his face. The incredible heat of the inferno lapped about him. Quickly, he snapped out the spell to negate it. The conflagration winked out. He rose to his feet groggily, thinking of the Elements in turn. He had faced them all and survived! The Ordeal must be over.

The Guardian appeared in the middle of the cave. He stood with his arms folded in silence.

Brack spoke defiantly. "You did not treat me as fairly as my brother," he rasped. "Surely he did not face such harsh tests as those you have subjected me to." His black eyes once again sought to look into the Guardian's hood.

"You are the Dark One's tool. If it was allowed, I would destroy you myself. But the Balance dictates that I cannot slay you."

The grinding tones echoed in the small space. The two faced each other like combatants.

"Perhaps you should try," Brack sneered.

With lightning swiftness, the giant leapt at him and seized him by the throat in a crushing grip. With apparently no effort at all, he lifted the struggling Elf into the air. Frantically, Brack attempted to use a spell, but his every try was blocked. It was as if he had no power at all. The Guardian would snap his neck like a twig. He desperately hammered at the Guardian's arms to attempt to break his hold, but it was as if he beat against the very rock of the cave itself. The pain of before seemed a mild discomfort as his body shrieked for air and release. Just as he was slipping into death, the giant hurled him to the floor. The last thing he saw was the great hand of his tormentor reaching for him and blotting out the rest of the cave.

CHAPTER VIII

SILVERON AND DARKMOR

The figure of the Guardian came out into the sunlight, followed by Brack, whose previous confident demeanour was conspicuously absent. As the brother's eyes met, Malin was surprised to see that Brack had been more shaken as he had been by the Ordeal. This gave him a small measure of satisfaction, as Brack had always seemed to dismiss him as an inferior.

"Well," said Goldwen, "It appears that we have two new 'Brothers.'" The wizard smiled at his own wit, and the group responded. All but Brack himself smiled, but he nodded and gave all a cold glance.

The Council faced Brack and repeated the greeting they had given to Malin. The King turned to the Guardian. "We thank you for your part in the testing of these candidates, and allow you to return from whence you came. " He beckoned to Willowen. "Please see to it, daughter."

"Yes, Your Majesty."

The Guardian bowed low before the Council, and again before Anarys. His deep voice rolled out from beneath the dark hood: "It is my honour to serve." The cowl turned to where Brack stood, and the Elf shuddered under the giant's scrutiny. The Guardian then came and stood before Malin. "Farewell, young Master," he said. Malin bowed to him, noting the smiles on the faces of the King and the Princess at this display of deference. The Guardian then turned and preceded Willowen into the tower.

The Eldest addressed both of them. "Now you must choose your new names, Names of Power that will be yours forever. The Naming

Ceremony will take place at the central court at the heart of the city tomorrow. Tonight you shall both have time to reflect on what names you wish to choose for yourselves."

Malin smiled at Goldwen. He already knew what name he would choose. Brack, however, did not seem to be taking much interest in what the Eldest was saying. Malin was surprised that his brother had been so badly shaken by his experience in the Tower of Sh'Kaarl. He turned to see the dark wall of *nightblood* behind him. He had also had his moments of panic, but he didn't seem to be as affected as Brack. He glanced over at his brother, and his look was returned by a scowl, but it seemed that Brack was still pre-occupied by what had happened to him in the testing. In the bright sunlight, the testing didn't hold as much fear as it had done. In fact, Malin wondered why he had been so frightened. The Guardian had been a shock at first, but after he had accomplished the Ordeal, the strange figure had almost seemed friendly.

As he thought of this, Willowen emerged from the tower and bowed before the King. "It is done, Your Majesty."

"Thank you, my daughter," replied Anarys. "Tomorrow, newly-fledged wizards, comes the solemn ceremony of the Choice of Names. It is the most important decision that you will make. The Name of Power, which a wizard takes for himself, should be a reflection of what he is."

Malin thought that Brack would probably choose a name that reflected his desire for power. Brack gave him an enigmatic glance. His face was unreadable, and Malin wondered what was passing through that cunning brain. No doubt he would find out.

Amberon felt the unseen presence of Malkaar begin to form about him. He looked about in trepidation. Surely the Council would sense the intrusion this time. He was both shocked and relieved when he saw that no one but he seemed to feel anything out of the ordinary.

"Suggest a Name to him . . ."

The Eldest looked over at the group, ignorant of the dark energy amongst them. *What Name?* He thought.

"Darkmor . . ."

Amberon's face paled. Darkmor had been the foremost pupil of the Dark One, and had risen to be second only to Malkaar as one of members the Black Circle. How appropriate that Malkaar should want him to take that Name of Power. *No! They will realise the connection!* He licked his lips nervously.

"Do it! . . ."

Against his will, Amberon dismissed the Council, and approached the young Elf. Goldwen had watched all of this in interest. He looked over at Telewen, who nodded imperceptibly. *So! The Dark One was here.* Try as he might, Goldwen couldn't sense anything at all, but he trusted the perceptions of his ally. He waited to see what would occur.

The Council all bowed to Anarys and departed. Goldwen and Malin stood there with Willowen and the King. They watched the Eldest approach Brack, who looked at him with distaste. Amberon cleared his throat. "I could give you some advice on your choice, if you wish it."

Brack's lip curled. The others were only too aware of Brack's disdain, but the Eldest did not seem to notice.

Brack's steely gaze pierced the Eldest. "I do not need your advice."

The Eldest was taken aback. His face became stony; his thoughts were roiling in his brain. He was stung by Brack's rebuke, and was furious that the youth had belittled him in front of Goldwen and Anarys. "So be it," he rasped. He bowed to the King. "Majesty." As he walked away his fists were clenched in rage.

Brack's gaze followed his receding form. "I believe that I can do such a simple thing for myself," he said. His eyes met those of the Princess. "Do you not think so, my lady?"

Willowen returned his gaze with a cool smile. "I imagine you could choose to call yourself anything," she said sweetly.

Goldwen and Anarys exchanged a knowing look; Malin rejoiced to see the haughty Brack rebuffed so effortlessly.

The gibe was not lost on Brack. His face became blank. He bowed low before the King. "Your Majesty, I believe I will go and think on my task." His eyes were on Willowen. As he straightened, his glance slid from her. As he turned away, his face was almost as angry as the Eldest's had been.

"Well," said Goldwen, as they watched Brack depart, "such a dramatic young fellow."

"He is no match for Your Highness," said Malin, and was gratified to hear her laughing merrily at his wit; Anarys and Goldwen joined in. At the sound of their mirth, the dark figure of his brother slowed, shook its head angrily, and then hurried on.

"I believe that we should keep a close eye on him, Sire," Goldwen said soberly.

"You think he could become a danger to us?" said Anarys.

Goldwen nodded. "I feel that both he and Amberon could be dangerous." He kept silent about Telewen's suspicions. He would tell Anarys himself at an opportune moment.

The King looked thoughtful. He knew that Goldwen was right. Amberon only considered himself. Now that he was the Eldest... He put such thoughts aside, and regarded Malin. "Malin," he said, and the youth came forward, noticing that Willowen's eyes were closely on him.

"Your Majesty?"

"I am pleased with your testing. You showed very intelligent choices in the Ordeal." He smiled at the boy's bewilderment. "Ah, yes. I was aware of all that occurred beneath us in the chamber. Shall I tell you how?"

Malin nodded, still befuddled. He couldn't see how the King could possibly know of such things; he had been alone during the Ordeal.

"Well," said the King, "you know of the Shaping that the Elves do with living wood, making buildings such as they are in Oakendean?"

"Yes, Your Majesty, Goldwen has told me of this."

"Then know that the members of the royal house are the only Elves who can Shape stone." He gestured at the towers and buildings that surrounded them. "I Shaped all of Algol in the distant past. This city is the only construction in the world of the Elves that is not Shaped from wood." He indicated his daughter. "Princess Willowen is the last of the royal line of Elves who are Shapers of stone."

Willowen smiled at Malin's wonder, and his heart leaped within him. "And," she said serenely, "I should like to add my congratulations to my father's. The Ordeal is very dangerous; only the strongest and the most worthy candidates succeed."

Malin bowed. "Thank you, my lady."

"Also," continued Anarys, "we have a pact with the Elementals. All of the magic of the Elves is based on the use of the forces that the Elementals command. But I imagine that your mentor will go into much further detail."

"I will," said the wizard. "The Elementals provide us with all of the powers that we draw on. They also help us in the Ordeal."

Suddenly, like a flash of light, it became clear to Malin. "The Guardian is an Elemental!"

"Yes," Goldwen said. "The Guardian is a manifestation of all of the Elements.'

"And he is called forth from the stone of the tower itself," added Willowen, smiling, and her smile was quite unlike the mocking quirk of the lips she had shown to Brack.

"The Guardian speaks to me in mind-speech. I can see that which he sees," said Anarys. "And so, I could follow your Ordeal."

"Then the tower and the Guardian are one?" queried Malin.

"Indeed," said Willowen. "His show of respect to you is a mark of esteem on behalf of the Elementals. He is himself the Ordeal, as well as a trusted aide to the Elven Kingdom."

"It is so," added the King. "And you are the first candidate in many years to use the proper responses to the Guardian's attacks. Many others passed the Ordeal, but they did it in many different ways."

"Who was the last to do this?"

Goldwen bowed.

"You!" said Malin.

"I am proud of you, my boy." The wizard clapped his hand on Malin's shoulder.

In the shadow of the nearest tower, Brack stood watching. He had not gone far when his curiosity stopped him: He wanted to know what the King had had to say to Malin. He listened in as he had done before, and as he heard what was said, he hissed venomously

"It is of no matter . . ."

Brack's angry face contorted. "It matters to me!" He shook his fist in fury. "They think I am a fool! I will show them all!"

"Do not let it concern you . . ."

The Elf lowered his fist slowly, still shaking with the violence of his feelings.

"Why did you not help me in the Ordeal?"

The cold energy swirled around him, chilling him to the bone. He gasped at its touch.

"The Guardian is too strong . . . He would have sensed my presence . . ."

"Then you are not *all* powerful," Brack sneered.

The intensity of the cold increased, crushing him in its icy embrace. Brack's breath smoked in the air as he shivered in the sudden cold that wrapped him in frigid folds.

"Do not presume to lecture me . . . I can destroy you if I wish . . . You will do as I command!"

The chill suddenly snapped off, leaving him gasping. "I . . . will do as you . . . command . . . Master," he husked through chattering teeth. The normal heat of the day returned slowly to his frozen limbs. Then, turning on his heel, he walked off toward the tower he had commandeered.

From behind some bushes in an ornamental garden, the Eldest appeared. He followed Brack out of sight with his gaze.

"Are you certain that the boy will serve?"

"He will . . . I will offer him power that he will not refuse . . ."

"But the others – Telewen and Goldwen –"

"Yes, Eldest?"

Amberon whirled at the sound of Goldwen's voice. The King, the Princess and Goldwen and Malin stood before him. His eyes went wide as he realised that they had heard him. Did they know that Malkaar's presence was amongst them?

He coughed nervously. The eyes of the four seemed to pierce him.

Goldwen came forward. "Is something wrong, Eldest?"

Amberon shook his head rapidly. "No. It is just that boy –" his voice faltered.

"He angers you?" Anarys said.

"Yes, Your Majesty." He bowed, hiding his eyes, fearing that he would give away the presence of the Dark One by the look of alarm in them.

King Anarys exchanged a look with Goldwen. The wizard nodded. Princess Willowen and Malin stood there silently.

Malin could sense the emanation of dark power that surrounded the Eldest. He was shocked that he could finally feel it. He glanced at the others, but only Goldwen seemed to have detected it. What could this mean? Did he himself also bear the taint of dark magic? He watched expectantly.

"You must master your passions, Eldest," said Anarys. "Are we not taught from childhood how to control our emotions?"

Amberon stood erect before the King. "Indeed, Sire. Please forgive me."

Anarys nodded. "I forgive you. I realise that the boy is dangerous and difficult to control. However, we must try to keep our own feelings under tight rein, or they will be our undoing."

For the first time, Goldwen began to sense something just on the very edge of his perceptions. He probed lightly in its direction. Tantalisingly, there came the faint suggestion of an unseen force. It *was* the Dark One! He let none of what he sensed register on his face.

Amberon bowed again before the King. "I shall, Your Majesty. May I suggest that I keep a close watch on the boy?"

"Yes. That is a good idea. You may go."

Amberon bowed to them all then walked purposefully away.

"Majesty, may I speak with you?" Goldwen gave the King a meaningful look.

Anarys saw the purpose in the wizard's gaze. "Yes," he said. He smiled at Willowen and Malin. "Perhaps you would excuse us?"

Malin returned the smile and bowed to Anarys. "Of course, Sire." He grinned at Willowen as Goldwen and King Anarys walked away. What a wonderful opportunity to talk to the Princess. "It seems we may have that talk, Your Highness."

Willowen laughed. "Do you think that your mind can concentrate on mundane things after your experience today?"

For a moment, Malin's face clouded as he recalled the Ordeal. Then he remembered the sensation of the unseen force that had surrounded the Eldest. He couldn't feel anything at all now, and looking after the retreating figures of the wizard and the King, he could sense the energy following them. He must tell Goldwen about it. He turned back to the Princess. "Nothing that you could say would be mundane, my lady." He was gratified to see her eyes shine with pleasure, and then he fell into step with her as they followed the others at a discreet distance.

"I believe that Goldwen has been teaching you other things besides magic," said Willowen. "You seem to be more at ease."

Malin nodded. "I do not understand. Before the Ordeal I was . . ." He searched for the words to describe how he felt.

"Unsure of yourself?"

He looked sidelong at her beautiful face. She had not changed. He still felt the same sense of awe at the sight of her beauty, but he wasn't intimidated by her presence at all; in fact, he felt very comfortable by her side.

"Yes. It is as though now that I have proven my powers to myself, I feel more confident." He looked ahead to watch the two figures of Anarys and Goldwen. He could sense the unseen energy around them. He wondered if Goldwen could also.

Willowen's voice brought him back to himself.

"What do you think of me now that you are confident?"

A playful smile was on her lips. Malin knew that she was teasing him.

"What do I think of you?"

"Yes, Malin."

Those wonderful eyes looked deeply into his own. His newfound confidence disappeared. He stumbled as they walked.

"Uh – I think that you are the most –"

Willowen smiled at his shyness. She raised an eyebrow in the same way that he had seen Goldwen do. It helped him to relax.

"Beautiful," he finished. He looked down at his feet; ashamed that he was still awkward when he spoke to her.

Willowen took his hand. Their eyes met. Her smile was one of warmth and compassion. "That is nice," she said. "Thank you."

His face burning, Malin only smiled as they walked hand in hand.

Ahead of them, Goldwen and Anarys were deep in conversation. Goldwen could still feel the power that enveloped them, but he didn't mention it.

"So you believe that Amberon is in league with the Dark One?" The King's voice was grave.

"It is a possibility, Sire. He has acted strangely since the beginning of these events, and Telewen has suspected the presence of some force."

"You have felt nothing yourself?"

"No, sire. But I trust Telewen. He was certain that there was something there."

Anarys reached out and took Goldwen's arm. They slowed to a stop as the King's voice lowered. "We must have proof, Goldwen. If the Eldest is involved with Malkaar, we are facing a very dangerous situation."

The wizard nodded. "It is not only Amberon that we should watch. Narwen and Korwen were supportive of his decision to make Candreen Master of Void Magic in my stead. With their backing, he can do very much what he likes."

"This could lead to a split in the Council," said Anarys.

"I agree. If the Council were to be broken, it would serve the interests of the Dark One. That possibility, and the unknown agenda of the wizard Brack must make our position one of great watchfulness."

They both turned at the sound of laughter. Willowen and Malin were enjoying each other's company. They were approaching the two grim figures, unaware of the seriousness of their discourse.

"Yes," replied Anarys. "We must not be taken by surprise." Then he smiled at the other two as they came up. His voice lightened. "I see that both of you are in good spirits."

Willowen's smile was infectious. "Malin was describing your teaching, Goldwen. " She glanced sidelong at Malin, and her tone became mock serious. "I think he is not happy with some of your tests."

Goldwen nodded, catching her mood. "Yes, he is a bit reluctant to show his real power." The wizard caught the King's eye. "Perhaps I should be a sterner task master?"

"Oh yes," said Anarys. "We must ensure his powers are fully awakened, whatever the cost."

Malin stared at the three, and then he suddenly realised that they were teasing him.

Willowen placed her hand on his shoulder as they laughed. "We know that you are a good student, Malin. Goldwen has gone on and on about your promising skills."

"Indeed," added Anarys. "It is the only thing that Goldwen has spoken about these last few days. He almost talked as much as a Man."

The wizard smiled. "They do love to talk. If only they would *think* more."

"Well," said Willowen, "You can be very proud of Malin. He has shown that he has the ability to become a great wizard."

"And so he shall," said Anarys. "Come." He turned and continued walking towards the towers.

Malin offered his arm to the Princess, who took it smilingly as they followed the King and Goldwen. He felt the dark force fade away.

Malin and Goldwen sat and talked in his new tower. They spoke of the many things that Goldwen had taught him about magic. The youth couldn't believe that he had learnt such lore in such a short time, and he was ecstatic that Willowen had spoken to him with such warmth.

"Do you think she likes me, Master?"

Goldwen smiled. "Of course she does."

Malin beamed at this.

"But do not forget who she is." Then, seeing Malin's crestfallen look, he continued: "Willowen is the Princess Royal, Malin, and you are dedicated to magic. Perhaps you can be good friends, but no more."

Malin's face fell. "I do not want to be dedicated to magic if I cannot be with her."

Goldwen nodded. "I understand," he said soothingly. "I also had to give up much for the position of Eldest. But there are some things which are not meant to be."

The youth realised that the wizard was speaking about his own unrequited love. Goldwen had never mentioned a name, but Malin had his own ideas who she was. Malin had been told that the Council members did not interact with women; it was something to do with keeping their powers within themselves, undiminished. When Goldwen had been the Eldest, he had been even stricter in the observance of this custom. Malin could not see how the love between two people could affect magic. He brought himself out of his musings. Goldwen was speaking again.

"You must understand that you and your brother were created by magic, and that there was Dark Magic in his making. I know that Malkaar was the Maker. And even if he has not shown himself to us, I know he has somehow freed himself from the Ice of Foreverness." The wizard looked grave. "I knew I was not powerful enough to face him and would be also unable to defeat Brack. You are the only one. And I believe that Malkaar will show his hand soon."

"But it still does not mean that I have to like the situation."

"No," replied the wizard, "But he must be crushed, once and for all time. If not, all Erathyn will fall into Darkness. Our time is ending, and the time of Man is about to begin. We must ensure that they are not enslaved or destroyed by him."

Goldwen put his hand on the youth's shoulder. "You will succeed in stopping Malkaar, my boy. I will assure you of that."

"I hope you are right." Malin looked thoughtful.

"What is it?" asked the wizard.

Malin smiled. "It was nothing important, Master."

"Tell me."

"It was just that I noticed the difference between you, and the other Elves."

"Yes?"

Malin shifted in his chair. "Well, most of the Elves seem to be very stern and unemotional, without –"

"Feelings?" supplied Goldwen.

Malin nodded. "Yes. But the King, the Princess, and you all have an easy going sense of humour."

"I think that it is because the Elves control their feelings: they are taught not show emotions. This does not mean that they do not have them. It was by doing this that they felt they were above the passions that ran unchecked in Men and Dwarves. It made them feel superior to them."

"Then why are you different?"

"The King, the Princess and I have all been in the company of the other races. King Anarys respects all Men and Dwarves; he has many friends amongst them. The Princess also is of like mind, and I myself have spent many years with all the races of Erathyn. I have learned that to be as proud and aloof as the Elves are seen to be is not a good way to endear yourself to the people of the other races who you would wish to be friends with." He chuckled. "I have also had a few arguments in Council about my *misplaced* humour."

"Will I be the same?"

Goldwen placed his hand on Malin's shoulder. "I gave you the same outlook as I have myself. Men can fear us for our immortality and our powers of magic. You will find that with a little humour you can make friends easier."

"I do not understand."

The wizard smiled. "You will."

Malin sat back in his chair. He glanced at Goldwen, and then looked away. The wizard knew that there was something else on the youth's mind. He waited for Malin to speak, but he just sat there, pointedly not meeting Goldwen's gaze.

Goldwen cleared his throat, and Malin reluctantly turned his attention to him.

"Is there something else you wish to tell me?" the wizard asked.

"No, master. I am waiting for further instruction."

Goldwen smiled knowingly. "Something troubles you. Tell me what it is. There should be no secrets between us."

Malin looked at his master. Surely he could tell Goldwen what he had felt? But what if Goldwen thought that there was some taint of Dark Magic within him? *Could* there be? No, it was not possible. His brain was wracked with doubt. Malin heard chuckling, and looked up.

Goldwen was sitting there, and laughing quietly to himself. He had been watching the agony of indecision flit across Malin's face. He held up his hand.

"I do not mock you, Malin. I know what it is that troubles you. You also felt the emanations of Dark Magic that Telewen told me about, did you not?"

The youth nodded. "Yes, master," he said hesitantly.

"But you were afraid that I would think that you were touched with it like Brack is," Goldwen stated.

"Yes, master," Malin said.

Goldwen smiled. "Put your fears to rest. I know that you are not like him. The power within you is for good, not evil."

Malin sighed in relief.

"However, there is a definite connection between you; it is the result of how you were created. Dark Magic was used, and that has left you subsceptible to receiving its energy and sensing whenever it is present. I too could sense something, but very faint. I cannot feel it as strongly as you and Telewen can."

"So you are not concerned that I could be like Brack?" Malin asked.

"No," Goldwen said. "You are complete opposites." His face grew thoughtful. "But this could prove advantageous to us. If you can sense when the Dark One is present, we can be on our guard. We can use this in our fight against him." He saw relief spread across Malin's face. "Have you had enough for one day?"

"No, master," Malin said, beaming. "Teach me more."

In the meantime Brack was sitting alone in the Eldest's tower. He had sat motionless all day; his face set in a dark, brooding scowl. He did not seek the company of others. Indeed, he didn't think that any of the city's Elves would enjoy his company, even that fool the Eldest. He didn't want his meddling advice on his Name of Power. Anyway, he thought to himself, *why* should he remain here? He knew he should be gone, but the Princess haunted him. He wanted her, but not as he had taken advantage of the girl Neldriin. He wanted her as she was, not as some docile puppet.

The Voice came to him, cold, evil, sending a chill up his spine.

"Come ... come ... I will give you power ... come to me..."

Brack's head snapped up at the sound.

"Where? – Where are you?" He couldn't sense anyone near. The Voice had promised him power before. But nothing had happened.

"See ..." said the Voice.

A red point of light appeared on the wall before him. The room was lit by only one candle, and this dimmed as the light grew in intensity. Suddenly, it expanded into a widening circle of fire, and Brack was drawn out of his chair, and he plunged into it. He gave a strangled cry. He was flying through the sky over a wilderness of mountains, rushing at incomprehensible speed. His hair and robes whipped about him as he hurtled through the air. His eyes watered in the screaming wind that battered his face. In his headlong flight, he was aware of the pounding of his heart, and he could clearly hear the tempest of his blood throbbing in his ears. In the distance, he could see a tall edifice above a valley filled with two battling armies. As he sped closer, it was apparent that it was a dark tower. He looked down, and saw the two great hosts locked in combat; they did not move, and he wondered at this.

He cried out again as he fell towards the tower. Expecting to be dashed to pieces against the wall, he closed his eyes and threw his hands before his face. Abruptly, his forward motion ceased, and his eyes flew wide in shock. The echo of his last scream of terror faded. His breath came in harsh gasps, and his heart hammered in his ribs with the violence of his headlong rush through the air. Sweat ran down his face and body. He was on his knees, shaking in fear as he looked about himself in amazement. A musty reptilian reek invaded his nostrils.

He knelt in a stone room, before a throne horribly made of bones. Upon it was the most wizened, emaciated creature that he had ever seen. The figure gestured for him to rise, and he did so, swaying dizzily. All was silent, and the room was dimly lit by only a few flickering cressets on the wall.

"Welcome, Brack." The enthroned one's voice was thin and husky. "I have been looking forward to meeting you." His eyes burned like the flames in a fire; always changing. These orbs regarded Brack intently.

"You are Malkaar?" Brack's mind spun with the evidence of the power required to transport him here. No doubt that this was the sorcerer's tower in the Kharden Mountains.

"Yes. Listen closely. You must come to me. I shall teach you the forgotten Dark Arts. Together we shall destroy the Elves and their feeble magicks. I shall be avenged, and you shall gain such knowledge that has vanished from the face of Erathyn." As he said this, he clenched his right hand into a fist, and Brack could hear the cracking of the sorcerer's knuckles.

Brack smiled at this. "Is this why I was created?"

"Yes," said Malkaar. "I am all that remains of the Black Circle. I created you to help me to crush my enemies. Together we will wipe out the Elves, and then all in Erathyn will worship us, or become slaves." The sorcerer's eyes flashed. "Or they will die." His face was vicious with hate, and his voice hissed like a snake's. Malkaar's bony hands writhed before him in dread anticipation of his desires. "You have completed the *Ordeal*, have you not?" A sarcastic sneer appeared on those leathery lips.

"I have," replied Brack. "But I do not think it is a fair test of my abilities." He recalled how much trouble he had had in the Ordeal, and that the others, especially Malin, had seen his discomfort. His face burned as he remembered.

"It does not matter," said Malkaar, "The knowledge which I will give to you will make the magicks of the Elves seem like the nonsensical rhymes of children."

Brack was suddenly sure that the sorcerer somehow knew about all that had happened in Algol. A sudden rush of hatred toward the Elves filled him. He wanted vengeance for the way they had laughed at his discomfort. He would show them. He would become the greatest sorcerer of all. He would come to Malkaar and learn all of his wisdom.

Malkaar seemed to read his thoughts "Do you wish to learn the Dark Arts?"

Brack nodded. "I wish it."

"Good. Then before you leave your *kind* hosts, I wish you to take the Name of Power that I shall give you. This Name was the one my protégé had chosen for his own. Many years ago, Goldwen himself destroyed him. In this way you will be giving them a message from me, and they will have no doubt that you follow me."

"Very well," replied Brack.

Suddenly everything shuddered. The figure on the throne gasped, and the room swam before the youth's eyes. A low moaning sound began.

"I...I am losing the ... the ...connection..." Malkaar shook uncontrollably. He looked weaker by the moment. Now the moan turned into a roar of sound, and strange light flickered in weird patterns across the floor.

"What must I do?" yelled Brack into the deafening noise.

The room rocked again, more violently. Malkaar impaled Brack with his burning eyes, demanding allegiance.

"T-Take the ...the name -" Malkaar broke off.

With a crash, Brack fell back into the room in the Eldest's tower in Algol. He sprawled on the floor. A thin, high scream of frustration accompanied him. It seemed that the sorcerer had failed to keep the connection open. The portal of light instantly contracted with a rushing sound to a point and was gone. The cacophony of sound was shut off abruptly as it closed. Then, in the silence that followed his return came a single word in the tone of the Voice.

"Darkmor..."

The candle's feeble light flickered and grew brighter. Brack's face stood out in bold relief as he rose. A look of satisfaction appeared on his face.

"Darkmor...I like the sound of that." He smiled to himself. He clenched his fist in an unconscious mirroring of his master's gesture.

In his tower, many miles from Algol, Malkaar looked at the image of the youth clenching his fist in exaltation. "Good." He said. Then he rose from his throne, evidently not at all fatigued by making the contact with Brack. It had all been a play designed for the youth's benefit. He waved his arm, and the image was gone. The room that had shook to the fury and thunder of sound and light was silent and dim.

The next day, the entire city turned out to see the Naming Ceremony. In the centre court, chairs had been set out for the Council, and two thrones were there; one for King Anarys, and one for Princess Willowen. They formed a semi-circle behind a waist high stone, amber in colour. This was the Naming Stone.

The Elves of the city gathered before the stone and waited in respectful silence. A moment later, the King's honour guard appeared, and the clear voices of their silver trumpets rang out, announcing the arrival of His Majesty. The host bowed low as the King, the Princess, and the Council appeared all dressed formally. They made their way up the stairs onto the platform. As the fanfare of the trumpets ended, King Anarys and his daughter were seated, and the Council followed suit. The crowd straightened and watched with interest.

"Bring the candidates forward," said the King.

Malin and Brack appeared. Goldwen accompanied Malin; Brack had Candreen by his side. Malin was nervous. Brack, however, seemed to have regained his poise. The two candidates advanced. Brack sidled closer to Malin.

"Do not be frightened, brother," he said, as though he was speaking to a small child. He looked out at the sea of faces and smiled. Malin was wondering about the change in him. Yesterday, he had seemed very angry, and Malin couldn't think of why Brack was in such good spirits today.

The Eldest came forward and beckoned to Malin. He walked forward, feeling all eyes on him. His heart pounded. He went over the speech in his mind. His mouth was dry, and he wanted to get the words right. He hoped that he wouldn't trip nor do anything embarrassing. Goldwen had told him the form of the ceremony, and had taken him through it, but to actually perform the rite itself in front of the whole city was very different.

In front of the Naming Stone he faced the Eldest, and spoke as clearly as he could: "I come before you as Malin. I have succeeded in all of the tasks set for me. I claim the right to choose a Name of Power." Good, he had said it right.

Amberon nodded, pleased with Malin's ritualistic speech. He turned to the Council. "Does the Council accept the candidate's claim?" he asked.

"We do," the Council said as one. The Eldest then bowed to the King.

"Does His Majesty accept the candidate's claim?"

Anarys looked Malin in the eye. A smile came to his face. "We do," he said.

The Eldest faced Malin. "Choose," he said.

Malin went forward to the stone. This part he was a bit wary of. He was supposed to hold the Name in his mind as he spoke, and the stone was supposed to display it somehow. Goldwen had told him about it, but had not been specific about exactly how it was to do so. He took a deep breath, swallowed, and felt sweat on his brow. Placing his hands on top of the stone, he said; "I choose the Name Silveron. Silver for purity."

The stone grew warmer, and veins like fire stood out upon it. Malin watched, entranced. Suddenly, a bolt of light leapt upwards and flashed above the platform. It resolved itself into his Name, written in silver on the air.

"Silveron!" cried the Council. Willowen's eyes shone as if she felt the thrill of pure energy from the stone, as perhaps she did, for she was a Stone-Shaper. Malin stepped back from the stone. The image of his name faded as he removed his hands, and the stone waited for the next candidate. The King summoned him, and Malin went over and stood by his side.

Brack had stood by while all of this had been occurring, seemingly lost in his own thoughts. Within his own mind, however, the Voice of Malkaar was whispering.

"Go forward ...Do not follow their ritual ...Ignore the Eldest..."

He walked up to the stone, not even looking at the Eldest. He placed his hands upon it. Amberon was dismayed at Brack's complete disregard of the ceremony. Brack's cold dark gaze swept over the Council, the King, and lingered on Willowen. He ignored Silveron.

"*I am ...*" began the Voice.

"I am..." repeated Brack.

"*Darkmor ...*"

"Darkmor," said Brack.

At this, a ripple of puzzlement went through the crowd. Goldwen and Anarys exchanged a concerned glance. The Councillors stood watching in silence, but there was a sense of unease surrounding them. Amberon's mouth fell open in shock. Silveron stood there in amazement. What was his brother doing?

The one now known as Darkmor turned to Goldwen. A fire of red and yellow flames appeared in his eyes. A steely smile wrote itself across his face. Malkaar's Voice suddenly came from Darkmor in thunderous tones; *"FOR NO-ONE IS MORE DARKER THAN I!"*

Willowen gave a gasping cry and fell senseless. The stone howled, and a black fire sprang up. A tongue of flame shot into the sky and then burst with a deafening concussion, which echoed across the city. There was a gasp from the crowd. The Name of Darkmor blazed above them in the heavens in roaring flames of deepest black. There was a sharp crack, and all turned to look at the Naming Stone. It had shivered into smoking fragments that lay scattered on the platform. There was no sign of Darkmor. He had vanished, no one had seen where; all eyes had been on the display.

Anarys and Silveron rushed to Willowen's side. The Elves stood stunned at the events. Only Goldwen realised the import of Darkmor's words, for had he not heard them before? He knew that Malkaar had intended him to receive his message, and to understand that he meant to destroy the Elves.

The sound of the stone's destruction reverberated and faded in the distance. The King's guard came to assist Willowen, who was still unconscious, her hands clenched in agony. Goldwen went over to the Eldest. He could sense the energy of the Dark Magic that had been present at the Ordeal. Of course, the Dark One would relish the destruction of the Naming Stone, and the confusion surrounding it. He probed the unsuspecting wizard, noting the distracted look on Amberon's face. Once again he saw the same evidence that the Eldest was listening to some inner voice. "Amberon."

Startled, the Eldest turned to him, clearly deeply shaken by all that had occurred. "Goldwen!" he said, "Did you hear? It *was* Malkaar. You were right." The Eldest's face was grim. In his mind, the Voice continued.

"Beware . . . He suspects . . ."

"Amberon, we must have a meeting with the representatives of the other races. Surely now you can see that this is beyond our control. Brack is merely the puppet of Malkaar."

"Agree . . . Confuse them . . ."

Amberon considered this. He had no wish to be involved with the other races, but today's events had disturbed him. He had had no warning that this would occur. Malkaar had not told him of this part of the plan. Grudgingly he realised that they must take part in what was to come. "Very well," he said, "We shall send for all of the ambassadors."

"And we must find him," said Goldwen.

The Eldest barked a short laugh. "I do not think we will be able to."

"Perhaps, but we must try." Goldwen nodded to him, and then went over to see what he could do for Willowen.

The Eldest gritted his teeth. *Why did you not tell me what was going to happen?* He could sense the presence still around him. His anger rose within him.

"Your reaction had to appear real . . ."

A sneer wrote itself across Amberon's face. *My reaction!*

The cold force intensified around him. He looked around quickly. No one else seemed to notice anything.

"You already know of Goldwen and Telewen's doubts . . . You must not reveal our agreement . . ."

The agreement. Once again, Amberon regretted his decision to ally himself with Malkaar.

"Do not forget who I am. Without me, you could not succeed."

The chill enveloped him in a crushing embrace. It ate into his bones with a frigid burning. Gasping within its spell, he looked up to see Goldwen staring at him, a puzzled frown on his face.

"Fool! . . . You are nothing. . . I gave you power over the Council . . ."

As he shivered and listened to the Voice thundering in his brain, he saw with trepidation that Goldwen was coming over to him. Perhaps the wizard could sense the Dark One?

"I could take that power away . . ."

As Goldwen approached, Amberon was struck with terror. If Goldwen felt the energy and exposed him to the Council, he would be finished. *Leave me! Leave me!* His thoughts were in turmoil, and his hands shook uncontrollably.

"You will do as I command . . ."

Yes! Yes! You must leave, Goldwen will sense you. Amberon watched in horror as Goldwen strode up to stand before him.

"Is something wrong, Amberon?" Goldwen could indeed sense the presence, but he kept the knowledge of it from his face.

The energy of the Dark One faded away. Amberon almost smiled in relief.

"Do not forget . . ."

As the numbing cold left him, Amberon met Goldwen's level gaze. "I am fine," he said. "It was just the shock of the Dark Magic."

Goldwen knew that the dark force had left the other wizard. What had the Dark One said to Amberon? He must tell the King. "Yes," he replied, "Brack is very powerful. We must find him."

The Eldest had regained his composure. "You mean Darkmor."

A feeling of unease rippled through Goldwen at the mention of that name. "Yes . . . Darkmor. Now we can be certain that he is the tool of the Dark One."

Above, in the Eldest's tower, the subject of their discussion listened in. They were afraid of him! Good. They would learn to fear him more. When he had learned all that Malkaar could show him, then they would see.

The power that had coursed through him was intoxicating. Not like his own. It was stronger, more intense. And the feeling of satisfaction of surprising them and destroying the Naming Stone had been delicious. He wanted to feel that power again.

"You shall ... When you come to me ..."

" I will," said Brack. "I want to show them all."

"The power shall be yours ...And all Erathyn..."

All Erathyn, yes. But first, Willowen. She would come with him. He would make her his slave.

CHAPTER IX

THE DEBATE AT ALGOL

The council hall was filled to capacity. The Council themselves sat in their places at the main table on the dais. The Eldest stood at its centre, with the Councillors seated on either hand. A throne for the King was off to the right, within the right hand wing of the table. Seated at his right hand were Goldwen and Silveron. The faced the chairs of the emissaries opposite them. There were four seated there. A Dwarf, nearest of the emissaries to the council table, and three Men. They had been provided with dignified throne-like seats on the left of the dais. Shelarindel and Malor had joined the group of attendants of the emissaries down on the gallery floor. On the King's left there stood an empty chair, usually occupied by his daughter. Some stared at the vacant chair beside the King's throne, in puzzlement, but most knew the Princess was with the healers, for she had not recovered from the shock that had destroyed the Naming Stone. Since this time, nothing had been seen of Darkmor, although he had been sought for everywhere.

Silveron's gaze took everything in. He stared openly at the strange figures before him. For the first time, he saw both Men and Dwarves, and he studied the differences between them, and how they were both unlike the Elves. The Men were quiet and subdued, and Silveron remembered that they had remained apart from the Elves for many years. Some of them even looked afraid, and cast nervous glances around the room. The Dwarves, however, filled their seats like images of stone. Below them the Elves of the city had come to hear and were packed into the huge room, usually so still and austere. Now it rang to the Eldest's voice.

The whole assembly listened intently to his summary of the events of the past few days; beginning with the magical conception, birth, growth, and testing of the twins. Throughout his discourse, he acknowledged Goldwen's conduct and praised him for his actions. To Silveron it seemed as if the Eldest's approval of his predecessor sounded slightly false, and in the well-turned phrases, he sensed that Amberon subtly reminded the gathering that although Goldwen had acted well, he was now only an advisor to the Council. Silveron noticed that some of those in the hall looked at him from time to time, and he detected many emotions flitting across their faces as they listened to the account. The Eldest's voice vaguely registered on his awareness; he was far too interested in the sight of the first other races he had ever seen.

Seated in a posture of brooding determination was a heavily built but short alien that Goldwen had whispered was a Dwarf-lord. His name, Brador, was respected not only by his own people, but also by every race. Brador's underground home was many days travel away, Silveron knew, so he must have started his journey before the Elves' invitation had been sent. What could be his reason for coming to Algol?

His long brown hair and beard were elegantly combed, and he wore a tunic of dark brown belted at the waist by a broad leather belt that bore a shield-shaped golden buckle decorated with intricate interwoven runes. His only other ornamentation was the several rings on his broad hands. Silveron knew only one thing of Dwarves; that they were famed as metal-workers and stone-masons. He noticed how broad and expressive both hands were, and could sense both power and craft in them. Although Brador's body was still as he listened quietly to the Eldest's account of the testing, those hands constantly shifted on the arms of the throne.

Next to him was a Man: tall, dark and clean-shaven. His slim figure contrasted the stockiness of the Dwarf. He wore a forest green tunic, and his hazel eyes bespoke his intelligence. Every now and then his gaze would travel to Silveron, but if he met the Elf's eye, he would quickly look elsewhere. Silveron could sense in him the fear that the other Men displayed. He was called Jarron, a chief of the Kandaran people of the forest, who had come at the request of the Elves to this conclave. Like Brador, he also seemed to have his own reasons for being there. Unlike the Dwarf, however, he seemed bursting with the desire to speak.

Another Man next to him was named Egon, the agent of King Munare of the Kingdom of Rewes. He was a slight figure, dressed in court finery, with royal blue shirt and trousers, and a long cape of the same colour. His long blond hair was held back from his face by a golden band. His feet were shod in black boots that reached his thighs. His hand toyed with a short silver dagger that hung from his belt.

The next figure seemed a barbarian compared to the others. He carried with him the elemental cleanness of the Great Plain. In his green eyes lay the far-seeing look of one who embraced the mysteries of nature. He was a gaunt Man, dressed in pants and vest that were made of soft leather, light tan in colour. On his feet were soft shoes made of the same hide as his clothing. His long, black hair hung in a plait down his back. On his face and twining around his arms were designs in many colours, which Goldwen had said were *tattoos*. Apparently they were important to his magic, but Silveron thought that they gave him a savage appearance. His fascinated gaze traced their lines and swirls. The only other decoration on his person was a stone pendant around his neck that hung from a leather thong. In his right hand he held a long wooden staff, painted with mystic runes and festooned with feathers and strings of beads on leather cords. He sat with the silent patience of the wilderness. This was Nomayon, the Seer of the Free Tribes. As he felt Silveron's gaze upon him, he looked up and nodded to the Elf.

The Eldest was rounding off his account of the past few days. "Therefore, my friends, it seems that the Dark Magic of Malkaar has indeed returned. The young wizard Darkmor has shown us that he has the same powers that our old adversary possessed. The destruction of the Naming Stone was a show of great strength. Normally the Stone could only be destroyed by one of the Shapers of Stone; that is, His Majesty, King Anarys, or one of the royal line." All eyes turned to the vacant chair. Silveron remembered that Willowen was a Stone-Shaper too. He wondered if she was all right.

Silveron sat silently during all this discourse. He stared at the Men and Dwarves. Their appearance fascinated him. Their faces were so different to those of the Elves. They were coarser, more lined and darker in tone. Their ears were rounded and not pointed like the Elves were, and their eyes were also rounded, not almond-shaped as his own. Their clothing looked unusual. Even their movements appeared alien to him. But they seemed to be firm in their convictions and beliefs. Why did many of the Elves hold only disdain for Men? The King's voice broke into his thoughts.

"We must find Darkmor and deal with him. Goldwen believes that Malkaar is behind all of this, and the Council and I agree with him. Somehow the dark mage is free again. For the sake of all Erathyn, we must face him, and this time destroy him."

A murmur of unrest spread through the hall. Silveron could see that the two well-dressed Men were also disquieted. The one called Jarron stood, obviously unable to keep silent any longer. Silveron noticed that the Man was uneasy in the presence of the wizards, and it was also obvious that Jarron was puzzled about something. All through Amberon's address, the Man had sent searching gazes at Goldwen and Amberon. Perhaps he wondered why Goldwen was not the Eldest? The frown written on his face seemed to show that he was surprised, even shocked to see Amberon in his new position of power.

He turned his intense gaze upon Anarys. "Your Majesty. I must speak. We are in desperate nedd of your help. Our villages are under attack." He came forward, bowing to the Council and the King. "In the last month, four of our villages have been destroyed, burnt to the ground, and all of their inhabitants put to death. These acts are committed by a unknown group of warriors who come in the night, none of whom have ever been seen. Even if any of their number are slain, they are taken away before the sun rises, and they leave nothing of their own behind, save dark blood."

"They call themselves *Schaaka*." Brador's rich bass voice came from behind Jarron. "This means Night in the Goblin tongue. They are from the darkest regions of the Underworld. They cannot withstand the sun, and even shun the torches that light our realm. They are not one of the Goblin clans that we have met in battle, but whence they come we know not. They strike from the shadows and disappear, only leaving the rune *Schaaka* painted with their victim's blood upon the faces of the slain. None have seen them and lived to tell what they may be. Mayhap they were part of the Army of Darkness centuries ago. Against my people too have they made forays, but our mountain strongholds have withstood them thus far. But lo, can we defy them forever? For they are very many. That is why I have come to the Council and the Elven-King to ask for aid. For if this is the doing of Malkaar returned, as we Dwarves believe, do not the Council and the Elven-King bear some responsibility therein?"

There was a ripple of restlessness in the hall. The ancient but unforgotten War of the Races was a matter of general contention. The Elves had been accused in the past of having been responsible for the rise of the sorcerer, as he had learned much of their lore and used it for his own ends. This knowledge he had taken back to the Black Circle, and not long afterward, they had made their bid for the domination of all Erathyn.

As Silveron looked at the Kandaran chief, he saw that Jarron was shocked by Brador's words. He was clearly shaken by what the Dwarf-Lord had said about the mysterious attackers. Why? The Man stared at Brador nervously, noticed only by the Elf.

"We are not here to point fingers, Brador, but to decide what is to be done." King Anarys held out his hand in a placatory gesture.

Brador bowed. "Your pardon, Your Majesty. Stories also have I to tell of the camps about the Tower of Malkaar, and the rumour that an army is gathering there. Some say that the ice that had held the tower has melted and vanished in the wind, where it had clung unchanged for so many years."

"I have heard something else of that valley," said Egon suddenly. "For there are Men in those mountains as well as Dwarves. Tribes which owe allegiance to my lord the King of Rewes. Our friends there have sent messengers to His Majesty who told a tale of a stone that fell in a great burning and thunder from the sky. It is said that the Dark One has returned to his tower, and that it is this stone which is the source of his new power."

"Vandaron went to the valley to see the truth," Goldwen said. "He fought the Dark One himself."

"Yes," Vandaron said. "It is true. The Dark One has returned. How, I do not know, but he is powerful. He defeated me, but instead of slaying me, he sent me to give a warning. He told me to tell all that this time he would be the victor." The Master of Birds paused, and then went on: "His army is vast; many thousands I saw camped about his tower. This stone I did not see, but there was the feeling of great power within him. Where it comes from, I do not know. Perhaps he has brought it down from the Void."

"Interesting," observed Anarys. "We must discover the truth for ourselves. If Malkaar is amassing an army, it must be stopped. We must also learn if Darkmor is indeed his creature. Vandaron, will the Avianinn help?"

"I do not know, Your Majesty. They have not been seen for many years. They prefer to keep to themselves." The brow of the Master of Birds was furrowed in deep thought. "I shall seek them, if you wish it."

"I do. They were always good allies in the past, and were fiercely loyal."

"I will have to find them first. They are always on the move, especially since their Eyrie was destroyed in the War."

At Amberon's left sat Candreen. He had basked in the closeness of his master, and in his new exalted position. From time to time, he had glanced at Goldwen, and when the former Eldest had met his eyes, he had smiled condescendingly. Now he spoke.

"Surely the Master of Birds can find his friends?" Sarcasm dripped from every word.

Vandaron turned at the sound of his voice. He held no esteem for Candreen, and was disgusted by the way he had come into his position. He noticed that Korwen and Narwen waited expectantly for his reply. Amberon also stood waiting, interested to see if Vandaron would be stung by Candreen's attitude.

The atmosphere in the hall underwent a subtle change. Even the Men there could sense it. Would these unpredictable Elves fall out among themselves at this dangerous time? Jarron, still standing before Anarys, nervously swallowed, and felt sweat break out all over his body. He was indeed afraid. For him, the only Elves he had come into contact with had been Goldwen and King Anarys. They had set his mind at ease with their acceptance of him. The other Elves however, especially the wizards, filled him with uneasiness. Like most Men, he feared their strange powers and immortality. Silveron continued to watch the Man, wondering why he was so agitated. No one else in the hall noticed, their attention was on the Council. Jarron felt the Elf's eyes on him, stole a quick glance, and looked swiftly away, unwilling to meet Silveron's gaze. What was he so afraid of?

"They are *our* friends, Candreen," said Vandaron, clearly irritated.

"Where are they, then?" The speaker was Korwen. He raised his hands and spread them in a gesture of inquiry. "Surely if they knew of these events, they would have come to us before now?"

Before Vandaron could reply, Narwen interrupted him. "They will not be found." He shook his head. "They have had their fill of matters that are far beyond their simple brains. All they wish to do is to eat and mate."

"I agree," said Korwen. "I have not sensed their presence for many years. The very air has forgotten them."

Candreen smiled to himself, relishing the Master of Bird's discomfort. "Even if you find them, they will not join us. Master Narwen is correct. They are little more than witless birds."

Tension filled the hall. All could see that Vandaron struggled to keep his anger under control. Would he react to the gibes of the others?

"Not so," said a clear voice. Goldwen rose from his chair. He strode over to stand before Amberon. As he passed the figure of Jarron, he gave him a smile and a reassuring look. "The Avianinn were created as simple creatures, it is true. But they are loyal and staunch allies." He fixed Narwen and Korwen in turn with a piercing gaze. "They can be relied upon, and I have faith that the Master of Birds will find them."

The two wizards sat back subdued, and Vandaron nodded to Goldwen, gratified for his support. Goldwen and the Eldest faced each other, a sense of power building between them, and then Goldwen bowed before him and returned to his seat. The strained air of the chamber abated.

Amberon seethed. Goldwen might as well have dismissed him as an underling. Even though he had given up his position of Eldest, there were some that still deferred to his words. Amberon had meant to humiliate Goldwen by offering him the position of advisor, but Goldwen had somehow turned it to his advantage. Also, Amberon knew that Goldwen still had the backing of Vairon and Vandaron within the Council. As he fumed, he felt the presence of Malkaar's energy around him. A quick glance over at Goldwen told him that the wizard was still unaware of it. The Voice came to him.

"Ask Jarron if the raiders could be the Schaaka . . . Watch Jarron's reaction . . ."

"These raiders," asked Amberon, "Could they be these *Schaaka* that Lord Brador speaks of?" He turned his stare upon the Kandaran.

Jarron met his gaze. Clearly, the Man was afraid, and was daunted by the power he could sense from the Elven wizards. He appeared to struggle for a reply to Amberon's query.

"No – Eldest," he replied, "That would not be possible."

Amberon raised an eyebrow. "Why not?"

Jarron looked even more uncomfortable. He licked his lips nervously.

The Eldest enjoyed watching the fear play across the Man's face. Perhaps here was an opportunity to destroy the idea of another union of races before it had the chance to begin.

"Yes . . . Create discord . . . Make them argue . . ."

From his place at the table, Telewen caught Goldwen's eye. The look that they exchanged told Goldwen that the other could sense the presence of the Dark One. He probed the hall himself, and could just feel something very faint. He nodded to Telewen.

The Kandaran chief looked around at the group on the platform. It was obvious that the answer to what Amberon had asked him would not be to everyone's liking.

In a resigned voice he finally said: "Because we have had a trade agreement with the Goblins for many years. It would be unthinkable for them to break faith and attack us."

A shocked outcry met this statement. The hall echoed to the clamour as voices were raised in outrage. Jarron's attendants looked about themselves in fear.

At last Silveron understood the Man's trepidation. All of the races hated the Goblins; from the very first they had fought with all who entered their domain. No wonder that Jarron had been afraid to speak.

Brador surged to his sturdy feet. "*What*! Know you that the Goblins have no honour?" His massive fists clenched in passion. "Always have we fought them, and you tell us that they *trade* with you?" His eyes flashed with fire and his breath came in angry gusts. The wrath that radiated from the Dwarf-lord seemed to fill the chamber.

If Jarron was afraid of the Council, he did not fear the Dwarf. He rounded on Brador, and the fire in his eyes matched that of the Dwarf's. "Not *all* Goblins are evil, Brador. We haven't had to fight them like you. I've never even heard of these *Schaaka*."

Brador crossed the floor to stand before the Man. Down in the gallery, the Dwarf-lord's attendants rose to their feet. A hushed air of expectancy filled the hall. In other circumstances, the sight of Brador glowering up into Jarron's face would seem almost comical, but all there could sense the rage between the two.

"Too many friends have I seen fall to the envenomed blades of the Goblins to believe that they would have peace with you. A ruse it is to lull you into a false sense of security, and then they will strike. Lo, even in my Greatfather's time, they were known always to be crafty and untrustworthy." His voice was low but was filled with emotion. The Dwarves were almost the opposite of the Elves; where the Elves would seek to control and suppress their feelings; the Dwarves allowed them free range.

Jarron gritted his teeth. Relieved that he could turn his fear into anger that had a target, he retorted: "We have no quarrel with them. One of our own people is a trusted advisor to the Goblins, and negotiates for us the trade that is essential for our villages."

Amberon smiled to himself. The reactions of both were predictable. It was easy to see how the races had fallen out and still distrusted one another. The Dwarves were stubborn and set in their ways; all they were interested in was to further their craft and to be left alone in their mountains. They cared nothing for the outside world. Men, on the other hand, thought that they were entitled to force their opinions on all others, even when they were not asked for it. As the youngest of the races, it made up for the sense of inadequacy that they felt when they looked at the long lives of the Dwarves, and the powers and immortality of the Elves, which frightened and angered them.

"Are you certain that they can be trusted, Jarron?" said Anarys. "There are still many of us here who fought against the Goblins in the War of the Races. I tend to agree with Brador."

Amberon fixed his eye on the chief. "What assurance do you have that they are not responsible for these attacks?"

Now the sensation of an unseen power grew in Goldwen's mind. He could sense it around the Eldest. Telewen shot him an imploring look; clearly he thought that they should confront Amberon now. Goldwen shook his head to indicate that they should wait to see the outcome of events. He believed that the time was not right, and the delicate atmosphere should not be tried further. He watched and waited. Telewen sighed in frustration. Narwen and Korwen had seen all of this.

Jarron turned from the angry face of the Dwarf-lord. "No assurance, Eldest, but the fact that we have traded with them for so long, and that they have accepted one of my own kinsmen as an advisor should demonstrate that they have no involvement in these attacks." He bowed to Brador. "I understand the anger that you feel, my lord. However, the Goblins approached my people with the offer to trade, and we have been doing so since before I was born. In all that time, there has been no trouble with them. They cannot be these *Schaaka.*"

The Dwarf-lord shook his head. "I cannot believe that they are not misleading you. They are cunning. For six hundred years have I fought them. Ever has there been strife between us." He indicated the king. "His Majesty will tell you of the eternal struggle against their evil."

King Anarys agreed. "It is true, Jarron. The Goblins and the Elves have always been enemies. They have ever favoured the Darkness, and they sided with the Black Circle in the War of the Races. But long before that, any contact with them was met with savage hostility."

Brador nodded in satisfaction. He knew of the Elven King's feelings toward the Goblins. Surely this Jarron would listen to his wisdom?

"However," continued Anarys, "Time may change anything. Only we Elves are eternal. The world changes around us, but we remain the same. There is a sensation of difference in Erathyn. I can feel that there is something growing; altering the shape of this world. Maybe these Goblins are an example of this change. Perhaps, Brador, they were not part of the Army of Darkness. Is it possible that they are only as they seem?"

The Dwarf's eyes widened. "Seem? Surely Your Majesty does not suggest that our age-old enemies have reformed their ways?"

"I do not know, Brador. But if it is as Jarron says; that his people have enjoyed trade with them for such a long time, perhaps they only wish to be left in peace, and could not be these unseen aggressors."

"I do not like it," said the Dwarf. "Every Goblin has bared his blade to me. I could not trust them."

"Please, my lord," said Jarron, "I assure you that there has been no treachery from them. My own people were wary at first. There was a great debate when the Goblins made their offer. Many did not want to accept it, and indeed felt much like you. However, it was decided that we would accept, and see what the outcome would be. Thankfully, they have held up their end of the bargain, and we both enjoy the trade which has ensued."

Brador's grim look softened. He liked the young chief; it was just that he had fought the Goblins for so many years that he couldn't believe that they could be friendly with any other race. "Well," he said grudgingly, "Perhaps these Goblins are not as the Goblins which we Dwarves have fought for many years. Strange it is still."

"Strange, maybe," said the King, "But perhaps they are tired of strife, and only wish to be accepted by others." He spread his arms wide, indicating the entire hall. "Many of us have strayed from the close friendship which our races once enjoyed. The War of the Races did much more than destroy lives; it also drove us apart, and now many of us fear and mistrust any who are not of our own race."

Brador nodded. He returned Jarron's bow, then he and Jarron returned to their seats. All there in the hall felt the truth of the King's words. Each race looked at the other, realising that what he had spoken of was the end result of the conflict that had involved all of Erathyn. An uncomfortable silence fell, as all were lost in their thoughts and memories.

Nomayon's staff tip struck the floor, once. The sound was like thunder in the silence. Then he stood and came forward. "Elf-King, Elf-Council, Dwarf-lord and Man-lords," he called shrilly, "A vision came to Nomayon in the night. Bid him speak." His staff thudded upon the floor and the beads rattled as he approached the Council. He bowed before them, and then did the same before Anarys.

"Sage of the Plainsmen, I bid you speak your vision," said the King solemnly.

At once the seer's voice deepened to a chant. His eyes glazed as he spoke of his vision. "Nomayon saw a great mountain range, and beyond it, a valley. In the valley was a black tower and about it were many campfires. Warriors swarmed around these campfires. They were evil Men and as dark as the night without stars. Their number was very many, like to ants in their nest. In their hands were terrible weapons, which they shook in the air and cried evil words at the tower. A dark figure, wearing a cowled robe all in black appeared at its top and spoke to the warriors. It did not shout, but all there heard. In the cowl, Nomayon saw eyes that burned with flame."

"Then the warriors swept out of the valley like a great flood and came to the Great Plain, bringing fire and slaughter to the world. Every city that tried to defy them was crushed, and all were struck down. The armies of every land were overthrown and cast to the winds, their banners trampled beneath the warrior's bloody feet. An awful wailing was heard across the land, and black clouds of burning cities covered the sky by day and night. The Sun herself was a red ghost that wandered weeping in the shadow of darkness that covered all of Erathyn. The mountains themselves were thrown down, and the seas heaved in torment and drank all of the Great Plain. Two eyes of eternal fire remained, and watched over all, and everywhere was blood... blood... blood..."

There was not a sound in the hall.

Nomayon's eyes returned to a lucid gaze, which he turned upon Anarys and bowed again.

"It is well known that your visions are warnings the wise may not ignore, Nomayon," said Anarys. "That was indeed Malkaar's hope. He dreamed that he would rule all Erathyn and it led to the war that all our races remember, and some Elves and Dwarves yet remain who fought in it."

Goldwen spoke. "Your Majesty, we must once again form an alliance with all the races. Alone none of our peoples can withstand the power of Malkaar. Only together can we finally destroy him."

Amberon's eyes flashed as Goldwen overrode his authority. It was *his* place to advise the King, not Goldwen's! This time he would not overlook the blatant usurpation of his office. With his hands clenched to trembling fists by his side, he drew breath to speak. The Voice stopped him.

"Wait . . ."

"Indeed, Goldwen." Anarys looked over at the emissaries. "You must regard yourselves as ambassadors for your peoples, with full responsibility to speak for them. We must waste no more time. A council of war will begin at once. Send messengers to your leaders to have our decisions ratified. We thank you for your information. In these days of the waning power of the Elves, we shall come forward, perhaps for the last time, to help Men. Lord Brador, our time, and the time of the Dwarf-lords, is ending, but Man's time is only beginning, and they should not be destroyed."

Even as Anarys spoke, Silveron felt a sudden chill. Something was not right. Again, he heard that evil whisper:

"Darkmor...Come to me...Bring the Princess...Come..."

A vision appeard befor the Elf's gaze.

He seemed to see Darkmor at the healer's tower. Two guards lay prone before him, unconscious or dead. Sweat started from every pore as he saw his brother spring up the stairs and throw open the door to the room where Willowen slept, watched over by two healers. In a few long strides he was at her bedside, and though his trancelike gaze never left her form, with a casual gesture, he sent one healer flying across the room to strike the wall with stunning force and slip to the floor. The other Elf seemed to cry out, and then she fled. Darkmor ignored her and looked down at the peaceful face of the sleeping Princess. He lifted her in his arms and strode purposefully to the door.

Silveron gasped in his extremity. He tried to speak, but could not. A dull roaring was in his ears. The Voice spoke again.

"Good...Come...Darkmor...Come to me...Bring her to me..."

Silveron had stood. As he swayed in the grip of the vision, he felt Goldwen clutch his arm. Everyone in the crowded hall was staring at him. Suddenly he realised that he had not sensed the presence, although it had been in the hall all along. The events and his intense scrutiny of the emissaries had distracted him.

"What is it? What have you seen?" Goldwen stared at his pale face.

"My brother... The Princess..."

At that moment, the great doors burst open, and the Elf in the vision ran towards them, calling out desperately: "Majesty! Darkmor – taken the Princess! Broke into - into the tower - struck down Aldar – I came -."

"Guards!" Anarys leapt up from his throne. "Councillors, use all your arts! Seek him out!" He swept across the dais to where the emissaries had risen. "Your pardon, my friends, we must leave you. He must not take her!"

The Council rose from their seats. Amberon exchanged a look with Narwen and Korwen that was not missed by Telewen and Goldwen. As they came around the table onto the platform, Goldwen stepped up before the Eldest.

"May I assist?" he inquired.

Amberon smiled into Goldwen's face. "It is a time for wizards, not advisors," he said haughtily. As the Council left the platform in a swirl of robes, Goldwen bowed to the Eldest, but his eyes sought those of Telewen. Telwen nodded, and Goldwen knew that he would keep an eye on Amberon.

Egon knelt before Anarys, proffering his dagger-hilt. "Majesty, let us help you."

Brador nodded, and Jarron bowed. The seer inclined his head briefly, though his eyes flicked to Silveron.

The King touched the dagger. "I accept your noble offers. Lead your own escorts. You may go anywhere in the city."

Brador's bass voice roared out. *"My hammer!"* He bowed to Anarys and stepped down from the platform to the floor of the hall. One of his attendants came forward, carrying the Dwarf-lord's war hammer. As he took it in his hand, the light of battle flared in his eyes. He turned and lifted it in salute, his teeth flashing in a feral grin. Then the group of Dwarves hurried from the hall.

The other emissaries followed suit; joining their own attendants and plunging from the hall, though with no clear idea where to go. They led their groups in tight units among the Elves, Jarron's Men now with a sense of urgent purpose written on their faces, replacing the uneasy looks of before. King Anarys and Goldwen were flanked by four guards, and left also; Goldwen was whispering in the King's ear. Anarys's face was set tightly.

Only Silveron and Nomayon remained on the dais, unnoticed in the turmoil. Though Silveron could clearly see the confusion about him, he could also, as with some other sight, still see Darkmor, with the unmoving form of Willowen in his arms. They were crossing the bridge before the city and heading for the forest. Behind them, the two guards lay prone, and the gate lay wide open. As he saw the Princess laying helplessly in Darkmor's grasp, he felt a surge of rage. Turning to see the green eyes of the seer deeply probing him, he stared back at the wild face, and was surprised when the plainsman lifted his staff and indicated the door, as though he could also see the Elf's vision. Silveron turned away, jumped down from the platform, and weaved his way almost unhindered in the crush. The seer's attendants stood unmoved by the rush of people. Silveron looked back to see Nomayon still standing on the dais. The savage figure was a mote of calm amid the haste that had fallen over the hall like a spell. The Voice came again.

"Bring her...Darkmor...Bring her to me..."

Silveron ran out of the door and raced towards the main gate of the city. Around him, the different groups milled in disorder. Horses stamped and neighed; a medley of confused orders was shouted, adding to the bedlam. Silveron could feel an inimical will that imposed this chaos upon the disorganised host, and shook his head, struggling to keep in control. Mounted guards and groups on foot seemed not to know where to go, but with his strange double vision, Silveron saw his brother carrying his lovely burden, and was filled with purpose. He raced towards the gate.

Arriving at the gate, he was just in time to see the distant figures of his brother and Willowen swallowed by the green forest. He ran down the road and crossed the bridge. His heart hammered in his ribs and his pulse pounded in his ears as he rushed after them. Soon he too vanished into the forest in hot pursuit.

CHAPTER X

IN THE FOREST

One moment the forest was alive with the many small sounds of its inhabitants; birds, crickets, and the rustling movements and cries and calls of other creatures which crawled and crept in its shadowy depths. Suddenly, the leaves parted as Darkmor pushed his way through the trees and stepped into the open with Willowen. Instantly, the sounds ceased as he looked across the very clearing where Goldwen had begun to instruct Silveron in the arts of magic.

He glanced back over his shoulder as he left the cover of the trees. Although he felt that he was protected by the spell that had hidden him from the eyes of any pursuer, a nagging feeling that he was being followed made him uneasy. Willowen lay inert in his arms; she had not regained consciousness from the spell that held her in its grasp. Darkmor could remember the sudden compulsion that had come over him, that had driven him from his hiding place and brought him to her side as she lay in her bed.

As he crossed the clearing, he was thinking about how he would make the haughty Princess bow to him. He recalled the rebuffs Willowen had given him, and as his face showed, dreamed of the most intimate revenge. His feverish eyes moved from the Willowen's beautiful face to roam the curves of her body, barely concealed by the light shift that the healers had dressed her in. He lifted Willowen towards his face, and leaned forward to sniff at the heady female scent that emanated from her, closing his eyes like a predatory animal, as he was lost in erotic fantasy.

The edge of Willowen's hand chopped fiercely into his nose. He cried out in surprise and pain and dropped her. She leapt up quickly, and aimed a kick at him. Darkmor, however, recovered with the speed of a striking snake. He dodged her kick and cuffed her to the ground. He stood trembling, anger suffusing his face. A stream of blood trickled from his nose, and he wiped the back of his hand across it. Darkmor looked at the crimson smear and bowed his head to her in mock salute. The Princess scrambled up, pulled her torn shift together, and glared at him with loathing.

"Thank you, my lady." His hands slowly rose in front of him. "My turn."

A blast of energy knocked Willowen down again. Darkmor laughed.

"Good," said the Voice. *"Darkmor...She has spirit."* He agreed. Once Malkaar had her, though, she would soon realise how weak she was before the sorcerer's dark power.

Slowly the Princess rose, and lifted her hands in a combat stance. He smiled disdainfully, and sniffed once as the blood from his nose dripped to the ground. "Is that the best you can do?"

Willowen's eyes narrowed with anger. Her right hand closed over the amulet hanging at her throat, her left hand came up with the fingers spread out and she pointed her open palm towards Darkmor. "Try this," she replied icily.

His look of contempt turned to surprise as he felt a tingling sensation begin in his feet. An icy sensation flowed upwards through his body. Looking down, he could see his feet turning to stone. *Of course!* The Princess was a Shaper of Stone, just like all of the royal line.

He tried to move, but already his legs were following his feet into rock-like hardness. He could feel his body beginning to stiffen. He ground his teeth in frustration. Willowen now wore a smile of satisfaction on her face. Would this be the end of him? He gasped as the coldness of stone reached his thighs. His head fell forward as he sought desperately for a counter-spell. His hands clenched into fists. Suddenly, the Voice of Malkaar came to him again.

"No! Push it out...Push, Darkmor..."

He obeyed, too frightened to do otherwise. He could feel the strength of his maker joined to his own. Two forces contended for his body. The tide of stone met the opposing magic, which tried to push it down and away. His breath rasped harshly as he felt the hardness constrict his chest. The weight of his stone-like form pulled at him. His heart laboured like a struggling bird, then seemed to stop as the tide of petrification crept ever upward.

Willowen's face showed the intensity of her efforts; she had never before felt such resistance. She swayed and pushed against the Dark Magic of the sorcerer, sweating and trembling with effort as she struggled to defeat his power. Their rough breathing was the only sound in the clearing as the magical combat grimly continued.

The tide of stone inexorably crept upward. Darkmor braced himself for his end. He looked into the face of his enemy, and was surprised to see pity there. He ignored it as the magic surged over his body. As he felt it reach his throat, he gave an incoherent roar, as miraculously, the magic ceased its takeover of his body. Suddenly, he could feel it flowing downwards again, and the life slowly came back into him. Malkaar's power had won the deadly struggle. The Princess's spell was finally pushed out of his body. Willowen staggered as her magic was turned aside.

Darkmor breathed easier as his chest rose and fell normally. His head fell forwards as his re-awakened body tingled with the pain of returning circulation. He clenched his teeth against the agony. The hardness flowed down out of him, and with a crackling surge, a large circle of grass around him instantly turned to stone. Darkmor sighed in relief. Then his head came up, and his eyes pierced Willowen like spears.

"Good. Now bring her..."

Willowen stared in disbelief. No one had turned a Shaping before! Darkmor and his evil master together were too powerful for her to resist. There was only one option for her now, but she was loath to take it. There was no one to help her. Her face set in grim determination.

Darkmor held out his hand in invitation. "Come with me," he said.

"Never!" The Princess closed both of her hands over the amulet, and snapped shut her eyes. Darkmor looked on in confusion. What

was she doing now? He strode angrily towards her, ready to tear off her shift and take her there and then, before he dragged her into the North and threw her at his master's feet.

Suddenly, he saw with a shock that *she* was turning to stone. The same tide of magic washed over her, much faster. Before he could reach her, Willowen was a statue from the soles of her feet to the top of her head; even her shift had become rock-like. Darkmor gasped in amazement as he reached out and touched her cold face, now unresponsive, hard, and chill. She had denied him. Anger flared in him and he struck the statue a blow that knocked it to the ground, and then sucked at his bleeding knuckles as he stared at the supine figure. Willowen's closed eyes shut out his furious gaze.

"Better...She can be carried...She has courage as well as spirit..."

Darkmor thought for a moment. He recalled how Malkaar had brought him to the tower. "Master, you could bring us both to you."

"No...I am not strong enough..."

"Darkmor!"

He whirled at the sound of the intruding voice and saw Silveron striding towards him purposefully.

"Ah, the hero." Darkmor smirked.

"What have you *done?*" The youth's face showed his anguish as he looked at the still form of the Princess. He bent down and ran his hands over the hard stone that she had become.

"*I* did not do it. She turned herself to stone. She did not want to come with me." Darkmor's mind worked quickly. If Silveron were here, then the others might not be far behind. He felt weakened by the struggle with Willowen's magic, and did not think that he could face them. Perhaps he could convince Silveron to come with him?

"Think, brother," he said silkily, "You should come with me. The King and the Council only want to use you for their own ends."

Silveron rose. He shook his head. "You know that Malkaar must be destroyed."

"Why? For the sake of *Men*? They are barbarians."

"Listen to him, boy."

"No," said Silveron. "I will not be your puppet like my brother."

Darkmor was surprised. He hadn't known that Silveron could hear Malkaar as well. His brother spoke again:

"Not only for the sake of Men. There are many races in Erathyn. The Elves' time is ending, and Man's is just begun. " Silveron looked down at Willowen. "We must get her to the King."

Darkmor ignored him. "Malkaar has promised me power far beyond that of the Council." He appealed to Silveron. "That power could be yours, too."

"The power of Dark Magic? Malkaar only thinks of himself. He used you."

Darkmor gritted his teeth in frustration. "Only to help me. He wanted me to bring her to him. If it were not for his power, it would be me lying there ." He gestured at Willowen.

"Help me take her to the King. He will release her from the spell." Silveron pointed back towards Algol.

"You are a fool...The Elves will be destroyed..." The cold tones of the Voice penetrated his mind, as Malkaar brought his will to bear upon him. He could feel himself falling into a sort of stupor.

"You and Darkmor will bring her to me..." A million angry bees buzzed in Silveron's head. He blinked furiously, his eyes watering. Darkmor watched and listened, expectant. Silveron's resolve began to weaken. As the smooth tones whispered into his brain, he turned to his brother, nodding in agreement, his eyes glazed. He must obey the Voice. But then Silveron looked down at Willowen and the sight of her inert body acted as a shock of cold water to his muddied senses. Love surged up within him, drowning out the insidious Voice. The power of the Dark Magic vanished. A frustrated cry of anger echoed in his mind. He shook himself as if he had just risen from a deep dark pool.

"No!" He shouted. "You will not have her."

Darkmor's eyes narrowed. Perhaps this was his brother's weakness. His feelings for Willowen were obvious. Darkmor looked around the clearing, and then leaned closer to Silveron.

"If you come with me, she could be yours. Malkaar only wants her for her magic."

Silveron stood silent.

Darkmor continued; "I am sure that he would reward you with her. I know that you love her."

Silveron shook his head again. "No," he said, "I will return her to Algol."

Darkmor sneered. "Do you think that she can return your feelings? As your precious *master* has told you, you are destined for greater things."

Silveron turned on him angrily. "What do *you* know of love anyway? The only thing you love is *power*."

"Love does not exist ... Only desire."

"Yes," agreed Darkmor, "When you say you love someone, you only mean that you *desire* them.

"No," replied his brother. "Love is real. You cannot change my mind. Either help me or get out of my way."

Darkmor clenched his fists. Silveron was a stubborn fool! There was only one way to deal with him now. Darkmor believed that he would enjoy it.

"I am afraid that I cannot allow you to do that," he said. He moved between Silveron and the way back to the city. He was slowly raising his hands, summoning power even as he spoke. "She must go with *me*!" He hurled a bolt of energy at Silveron. Silveron was knocked flying through the air, landing many feet away. His breath left him as he crashed to the ground.

Silveron tried to rise, but as he did, another blast hurled him away again. He rolled along the grass. His eyes watered, and he coughed painfully. Darkmor's laughter stung his ears. It was echoed by the laughter from Malkaar in both of their minds.

"Where are your powers? Show me! Defend yourself!" Darkmor advanced, hands outstretched. Silveron shook his head; there was a great roaring in it. Another violent discharge sent him crashing through the saplings at the clearing's edge.

"Defend yourself!" Darkmor cried.

Suddenly Silveron had a flash of that day when Goldwen had used those very words in this clearing. He staggered to his feet. Blood from a dozen cuts on his face stung, and his body ached from the battering it had taken.

Darkmor advanced, confident in his power. "You disappoint me, *brother*," he hissed. He raised his hands to deliver a fatal blow. "Perhaps Malkaar would not find a use for you, after all."

"Destroy him," commanded the Voice.

In his mind, Silveron constructed the Ten-Fold Mirror as Goldwen had shown him.

Darkmor struck. The spell rebounded, flinging energy away from Silveron. Trees around him shattered into fragments, as the shock wave expanded outwards in a rush of heated air and energy. The ground was ripped up, and Darkmor was flung away into the clearing. He hit the ground heavily and lay still. Silveron staggered to his feet and stumbled towards him as a storm of leaves and broken branches fell around him out of the ravaged air. Darkmor lay face down not far from Willowen.

As he reached Darkmor, Silveron leaned down to see if he was still alive. It was a mistake. With a snarl of animal hatred, Darkmor flung out his hand. A ray of powerful force sent Silveron reeling.

Darkmor heaved himself to his feet. His robes were torn, and his nose was bleeding profusely. He raised his hands, conjuring forces between them. With a wolfish grin, he released a ball of fire at Silveron.

This time, Silveron used the Shield, and the fireball struck it and glanced off, merely staggering him. The ball spun into the forest and exploded into flame.

Up till this point, Silveron had only defended himself. Now he saw that he had no choice but to attack. A bolt of lightning left his hand and sped towards Darkmor. The bolt hit Darkmor's own Shield and crackled and hissed against it before being dispersed into the ground, which smoked and cracked.

"Not bad," said Darkmor sarcastically, "I was beginning to think that you had forgotten everything that fool Goldwen had taught you." They began to circle each other, trying to anticipate any attack. The trees at the edge of the clearing burned where the fireball had struck, and the crackling of the fire was the only sound as they stalked each other.

"I have not forgotten that you are the tool of Malkaar," replied Silveron. He was wary of Darkmor's words, and watched him closely. His eyes strayed to the clearing's edge. Surely their fight had been heard? Someone would appear soon. He need only prevent Darkmor from taking Willowen. He looked over at her whenever she was behind Darkmor.

"Not *tool*, say rather *apprentice*. I will learn everything that Malkaar knows, and his knowledge of the Dark Arts is vast." Darkmor was aware that Silveron had glanced at the Princess as they circled. The next time she was behind him, he would act. Better she be destroyed, than leave her to Silveron. If Malkaar could not have her, and ultimately Darkmor himself, then no one would.

As he saw Silveron's gaze pass him to the form of Willowen, he acted. Casting a fireball at Silveron, he leapt to the Princess's side.

But Silveron had seen the intent in his eyes, and had dodged the fireball. It smashed into the ground. Clumps of dirt fell through the air. Rushing forward, he flung Darkmor aside with a stroke of lightning. He stood astride Willowen, prepared to guard her with his own life. Darkmor got to his feet, just as King Anarys and his guard entered the clearing. Nomayon, and Goldwen were with them. Captain Nilda led a group of her bowmays behind them, and they unslung their bows and fitted arrows in a lightning fast move.

Anarys stared at the petrified form of Willowen and gasped. Nomayon came forward, chanting and shaking his staff. There was a shirring of swords as the guards advanced. Goldwen raised his staff, and a nimbus of blue-white fire gathered at its tip. Nilda and her bowmays took aim at Darkmor.

Darkmor saw his certain defeat at such overwhelming odds. Mere arrows and swords he didn't fear, but Goldwen... He hissed in impotent rage.

"Leave them...Come to me..." Malkaar's Voice sounded displeased.

Darkmor turned on Silveron again, his hands one above the other. He separated them slowly, conjuring a flame between them. "I am not strong enough to destroy you now, *brother*, but I assure you, I will return." Within his cupped hands, he had created a huge ball of fire that now spun with destructive force between his fingers. With a shout, he cast it at Willowen and Silveron.

It struck Silveron's Mirror and exploded into an intense flare of crimson light, blinding all in the clearing. When the glare had faded, Darkmor had gone. Silveron and Willowen were unharmed.

Anarys came forward. "She must be taken to Algol. What she has done is very dangerous." He nodded his thanks to Silveron. "You have done very well, Silveron. I thank you for the life of my daughter. Goldwen's faith in you has been justified."

Silveron bowed to the King. As he rose, they all turned to see Nomayon stride over to where the fire still blazed fiercely, threatening a large area of the forest. What was the Seer going to do? Above the roaring flames, they could hear him chanting as he approached the conflagration. Silveron gasped in shock as Nomayon stepped fully into the fire, placed his staff-tip into its heart, and sang briefly. In moments, the fire died down from a raging inferno to a flickering flame, then to nothing. The Seer strode back to the group, and bowed to the King, who returned his bow with a smile. Silveron looked on in amazement.

At Nildas's command, the six bowmays gathered the sturdiest of the broken branches that lay strewn about them. They tied them together with spare bowstrings, and placed the petrified Willowen on the stretcher they had improvised.

"Your Majesty," said Silveron, "Darkmor said that he was taking Princess Willowen to Malkaar, and that Malkaar wanted her for her magic. Why?"

"I do not know," said Anarys.

Nomayon spoke. "Stone from sky, Elf-king. Nomayon sees Dark One's mind. Great power locked in stone. Princess can unlock it."

"It could be, Your Majesty," added Goldwen. "Using the powers of a Shaper of Stone, Malkaar could learn its secrets. Only you and Willowen could do this."

"You could be right," Anarys said. "Forgive me, I must attend to my daughter."

Silveron and Goldwen bowed to him.

The King gestured to his guards to return to the city. The captain's bowmays lifted the unconscious form, and with the King's guard, proceeded across the clearing. Anarys walked beside Willowen's stretcher, his gaze never leaving her.

Goldwen clapped Silveron on the shoulder. "Well done." The young wizard blushed. "You have shown great courage, and you wielded your powers well. I am proud of you."

Nomayon nodded in agreement with Goldwen's praise.

Silveron smiled at the congratulations, but turned to look back at the clearing as they headed back to Algol. He'd beaten Darkmor this time, but he knew he would confront him again.

Crouched low in the trees, Darkmor watched them leave. The burning anger that he felt included the entire group. He would go to Malkaar, learn all of his forbidden arts, and then return and destroy them! *All of them!* Darkmor rose and turned away from the Elven city, heading towards the tower that lay far in the North. He could sense that his maker was not pleased with him, but he would impress him when he next met the Elves and his brother in combat.